Bond of Three

Emeka Obi

iUniverse, Inc.
Bloomington

iUniverse books may be ordered through booksellers or by contacting:

iUniverse
1663 Liberty Drive
Bloomington, IN 47403
www.iuniverse.com
1-800-Authors (1-800-288-4677)

ISBN: 978-1-4502-8301-4 (sc)
ISBN: 978-1-4502-8302-1 (hc)
ISBN: 978-1-4502-8455-4 (ebook)

Printed in the United States of America

iUniverse rev. date: 05/18/2011

To my mother, Maria Obi (1939-1989), thank you for the pure maternal love you provided me throughout those tender years.

Chapter 1

It was his first assembly in the new school. Onyekachi was in the queue with the other students, wearing his odd school uniform, which consisted of a white shirt with white khaki-like shorts, whereas the other students around him wore light blue shirts with dark blue shorts. He felt odd and shy for two major reasons: a number of students in the assembly hall were stealing glances at him, which was not unusual; and the new school was coeducational, unlike his former school, which was an all-male secondary school as well as a boarding school.

Boarding life was regimented. The former school enclave was a community of its own. Everything the students needed was found within; hence, there was no need for any student to leave the school vicinity. In extreme cases, in order to leave the school vicinity for some serious reasons, permission was obtained from higher authorities, and a stipulated time would be given for the student to report back to school. Not doing so would lead to severe punishment. Visitors were not allowed regularly, only on visiting days. Students were not allowed to interact with people in the surrounding communities. To ensure that that was not an issue, a barbed wire fence surrounded the massive area occupied by the school. As if to isolate the students more, the school was located beyond the outskirts of the urban area.

It was all different here, which meant that Onyekachi would definitely need an adjustment to his way of life.

For the more than one and a half years that Onyekachi was in his former school, his relationship with girls was affected. The biased nature of most activities did not help the boys socially, as there were no girls to play feminine roles. He got used to mingling with boys so much that he hardly socialized with girls, even during the holidays. One would wrongly think that he hated girls.

His mother, Mrs. Ezinne Ikem, had told him that there was nothing to worry about as far as changing schools, assuring him also that his new school uniform would be ready in a couple of days.

Onyekachi would not dare ignore what his mother said for any reason, so he accepted all she said without question, although he would have preferred to wait and start school when the new school uniform was ready. He treasured his widowed mother so much. Since his father's death the previous year, which was largely responsible for the transfer, he resolved to make his mother constantly happy in whatever capacity he could. Any act of stubbornness could cause her grief and indirectly remind her of her husband's death, which was still very fresh in her memory.

"We shall start this morning devotion by singing hymn number one seventy from hymnbook *Ancient and Modern,*" announced a fair-skinned girl who was to conduct the morning assembly from the podium. From where she stood, everyone had a clear view of her. Another girl, standing adjacent to Onyekachi, intoned the song, and others joined in immediately. The assembly hall was filled with the melodic sound of voices as they sang. After the hymn, the same girl who had conducted rendered a reading from the Bible. The principal of the school, Mr. Uche Dibia, who stood behind the students with some of his academic staff, moved up to join the girl on the podium. He was to speak and elaborate on the portion read from the Bible.

It was Monday, which meant it was the day for "the principal's assembly," when the principal himself delivered moral instruction. Mr. Uche Dibia was made the principal of Umuagu Secondary School after the introduction of the 6-3-3-4 educational system by the government. This system of education required that one spent six years in the primary school, three years in the junior secondary school, another three years in the senior secondary school, and a minimum of four years in a tertiary institution.

With the introduction of this educational system, some secondary schools like Umuagu Secondary School (USS), and a few others were converted to junior secondary. A few others were retained as senior secondary, while quite a large number retained both junior and senior secondary status. The conversion was based primarily on the population strength of each school. Usually, schools with lesser populations were mostly converted to junior secondary. With increasing populations, some of such schools would later retain their original status of either senior secondary or both junior and senior secondary. Mr. Dibia, close to retirement, preferred the USS, which was an easier school to handle. Mr. Dibia was an enormous and fatherly man. He was pious in nature.

"The portion read from the Gospel according to Saint Luke," said the principal, "is called 'The Parable of the Good Samaritan.' So, students, what is a parable?"

The unexpected question caused an immediate hush among the students in the assembly hall. None of the students seemed to have a befitting definition of a parable. It was common among the students to be extremely quiet whenever a perceived difficult question of this sort was asked. Nobody wanted to do anything that may attract the principal's attention and prompt him to throw the question at him or her. To the students, it was better to remain unnoticed than to fumble while attempting to answer. A wrong answer might give any student a powerful and long-lasting nickname coined from his or her answer to the question. In the past, some had gotten their nicknames through similar circumstances. But it was always different for a brilliant answer, as an accolade was given to the student.

"*Ehenn?*" the principal asked further, which was a local interjection used sometimes to inquire something or express delight.

Onyekachi could not bear the silence any longer, so he summoned courage and raised his right hand. The principal looked in his direction.

"Yes?"

"A parable is an earthly story with a heavenly meaning," he answered.

"Good, son! Oh ... the new student?" the principal said. He explained further: "A parable consists of a lesson or lessons to be learned from some familiar events in the world around. It is a story of comparison that requires deep thought and understanding. It is a story that connects the earth with heaven.

Whenever he explained anything, Mr. Dibia had a way of getting people interested. He was a good motivational speaker. As he explained, the place became quieter.

"'The Parable of the Good Samaritan,'" he continued, "teaches love and kindness to your neighbor. Your neighbor is one who offers a helping hand when you are in need or suffering with pain, as the Samaritan did. Your neighbor is not necessarily the person living close to you, and would keep away from you when problems come. The parable teaches works of mercy to people, particularly when they are helpless and need a helping hand. Helping is an act of love. You students must learn to help one another when the need arises. If you allow love to reign in your hearts, you will experience joy in helping one another."

The principal had a way of interpreting portions of the Bible with simplicity so everybody could understand, like some ministers did. The teachers and students alike admired him for that. He wanted to take after his late grandfather, Chikadibia, who was a minister of God. As a boy, Mr. Dibia's grandfather became interested in the activities of the early missionaries who arrived in their community. He drew closer to them and assisted them. In return, the early missionaries also spent time and resources empowering him. They gave him formal education. He was the first son in his community to travel to the white man's land. He lived in England for so many years that he married late compared to his age-mates. Some people said that it was because there were few black women of African origin in England at the time. After he was ordained a minister of God, he arrived home. When he came back, people said he spoke English through the nose like the white man. He later took a wife and had a family, which was the source of Dibia's extended family. He passed education on as a legacy to his children, who also passed it on to their own children. The Dibia family was popular and was known to have produced prominent men and women in the society. The family was large and had people of high social class from different occupations and professions.

Mr. Uche Dibia's theological training had made him convincing. It was a twist of fate that he finally landed in the teaching profession. Everybody in the school, including the nonacademic staff, respected him a lot for his piety and discipline.

After moral instruction was the prayer, which was followed by singing and recitation of the national anthem and national pledge, respectively. The formal salutation by the students followed it, with the signal coming from the bell rung by the conductor.

As he usually did, Mr. Uche Dibia gave some instructions pertaining to the activities to be carried out in the week. He was quick to remind the students that anybody who committed any serious offense would be suspended or expelled. The students never doubted whatever he said because he was always true to his word.

After the principal concluded, he left the assembly hall with the teachers. John Tasia, the school's senior prefect, came up to the podium and took charge.

"I want to seize this opportunity to remind you again that your noisemaking is becoming unbearable," said John aloud, mainly referring to those in the lower classes.

The remark was followed by an unruly noise, as if already planned by the lower classes. The other prefects intervened almost immediately, dispersing themselves in an attempt to single out the culprits. The place was quiet again.

The senior prefect continued. "Starting today, I want all class prefects to forward to me the names of the noisemakers for punishment; failure to do so means that they will be held responsible for noisemaking in their respective classes."

Some hisses were heard here and there, in a manner that would not allow anyone to find their particular sources. In this particular type of school setting, it was not uncommon to find some students from the lower classes who wanted to rub shoulders with the prefects and even challenge their authority. When the prefects tried harder to find the culprits once again, the hisses died down.

"Now, you can go back to your classes … and don't forget that the sanitary prefect will be around to check the areas you were individually assigned to sweep. As the others leave, I want the class prefects to stay behind for a brief meeting with me," said John authoritatively.

The students started to leave the assembly hall in single file, starting from the higher classes to the lower ones. Onyekachi and other members of JS2A moved into their classrooms.

He thought of his former school. Here in the new school, things were done differently. In his former school, no hymns were sung during the morning assembly. The prayers said were of two kinds: Islamic and Christian. That was to demonstrate the major difference in religion between the North and the East. Whereas the East was made up predominantly of a Christian population, the North had a majority of Muslims and a minority Christian population. It pleased Onyekachi that he was able to see and even interact with the principal on his first day in the new school. It was not a common experience in his former school. The VP administration or VP academic was there most of the time to attend to students in the vastly populated school. Though USS was a junior secondary school, students showed much disrespect to their school prefects, which was unlikely to happen in his former school, where prefects were not only respected but feared. Perhaps those were among the major differences between a community school and a big urban boarding school.

When he reached the classroom, he sat on his stool by his locker, waiting for classes to commence. One thing that Onyekachi did not realize, however, was that his answer to the question asked by the principal in the assembly hall had earned him the admiration and recognition of the teachers who were present at the morning assembly.

As he sat on his seat not talking to anybody, he was thinking of Nneoma.

Chapter 2

Nneoma was from the same village as Onyekachi. She was beautiful, just like her mother, Odirichi. Urediya, as Odirichi was fondly called, was regarded by many as the most beautiful woman in the village. When she was a full-grown girl, they said that any man who came across her must turn to see her beautiful shape from behind after having admired her beauty from the front. This was before her marriage to Nicodemus.

Because of her enormous beauty, people preferred to call her Urediya—the pride of her husband. They later chose to make the name cute and short: Ure. As she was a married woman, men had to control their excessive admiration of her beauty.

Ure and Dee Nico—as her husband was fondly called—had had five sons before Nneoma, but she was the only surviving child. Ure died when Nneoma was barely two, making Dee Nico a widower. Some people said that Ure made a covenant with her personal god, *chi*, to spare Nneoma, thus exchanging her own life for Nneoma's. Others said that it was out of sheer luck that the poor girl survived, while others said that she prayed to God more seriously to spare Nneoma.

None of Ure's previous children lived more than seven years before dying. Because of the circumstances of the deaths of Nneoma's previous siblings, certain people were quick to refer to her as *ogbanje*, notwithstanding the modern age. They had never expected her to live longer than any of her dead siblings, but Nneoma was thirteen and full of life. Her beauty, charm, and occasional spontaneity also helped buttress the point for such people as some of the attributes of an ogbanje child aside from early death. There was so much gossip about her. Some people argued that since her mother did not make it, there was more to her survival. Yet Nneoma refused to let the insinuations bother her. She continued to prove her detractors wrong by excelling in whatever she did. She was friendly and smart. Determined and courageous, she was also down-to-earth. She shone academically too. People, who were somewhat scared of her initially, began to wish she were their daughter.

Onyekachi could remember vividly that during the family stay in Kaduna, his mother once visited home and came back with news making the rounds in the village. It was about Nneoma's academic prowess.

"That Ure's daughter," she had said, "is brilliant. She made the best result in the Common Entrance Examination in her school. It was even said that her result was among the best in the entire state. I have always been impressed with the girl. She's refused to be weighed down by all the fabrications about her."

Onyekachi was not surprised. He'd known the potential in Nneoma when they were together in primary one through to primary three, before he'd left home for Kaduna. He only wished he were at home at the time to convince his parents, particularly his mother, that Nneoma was beatable after all. He remembered with a smile what happened when he was still at the village and in the same class with Nneoma. It was after their third-term promotional examination to primary three (he was usually in the same class with Nneoma). She had beaten him to the first position, and he'd nearly cried his eyes out. He denied himself food for the remainder of the day and thereafter promised himself never to allow it to happen again. Subsequently, he maintained first position in the class, with Nneoma always coming closely behind, until he left the school. He believed that first position in class was his birthright, and the only threat to it was Nneoma, his only rival. Sometimes the struggle for academic superiority made them quarrel for no justifiable reasons, like a couple would. Funny enough, those quarrels also boosted their intimacy. They also played pranks and did so many things together. Childhood days! That may be history for now, but he had not forgotten, and he hoped Nneoma had not forgotten either.

It was 7:55 a.m. on Onyekachi's digital watch. Classes commenced in five minutes. A few students who could not come early enough to clean the areas they were assigned to sweep before the morning assembly were still outside cleaning with the few minutes left. The sanitary prefect carried out general inspection of the portions. Because he was a new student, no portion had been assigned to him yet.

By eight o'clock, the classroom was almost full to capacity. Onyekachi quickly observed that some students in the classroom had already formed groups of twos or threes and were probably discussing him. He could only faintly remember a few faces.

"Is he a new student?" somebody behind him asked.

"Are you blind?" another replied. "Couldn't you have noticed from his uniform that he is new, or have you been seeing him around?"

"Chinwe, please don't mind Tony," another party added. "He's kind of asking silly questions nowadays."

Onyekachi was naturally a shy boy and detested such situations, especially with no familiar person around to keep him company. *Why*

in the world did Nneoma decide to abandon me in this classroom? he wondered
to himself.

Nneoma had assured Onyekachi that all was fine in her school
and had promised to keep him company. They had grown up together
in the early years, so she knew Onyekachi's weaknesses to an extent
too. If she had been around to keep him company in the classroom,
he wouldn't have minded if all eyes were on him. His mind reflected
to what had happened the day before.

They were discussing freely. Their discussion ranged from
academic life to social life, from language to culture and religion.
Most of the time, Onyekachi was on the telling side because of his
experience of having lived in both the North and the East. Having
never had an opportunity to visit or live in the North, Nneoma
was therefore more on the listening side. He narrated to her how
certain things were done differently in the North. In particular, he
emphasized, among others, an incident he would never forget.

While living with his parents and siblings in Kaduna, Onyekachi
had become friends with a Hausa boy named Musa. At the time,
he had yet to understand fully the religious and cultural life of the
dominant Hausa Muslims. He had never wondered why men were
more often seen in the streets than women were. They usually wore
caftans or *babanriga*. Only a few women, mainly those well advanced
in age, were seen—but not without their veils. Onyekachi and Musa
were in the same class, and he had kept him as a close friend. Musa
was among the few who enrolled in school and persevered to the point
of nearly completing his primary education. And he still wanted to
go much further.

Musa was helping him learn the Hausa language. It was obvious
that one had to learn the language in order to integrate fully into the
society. A majority of the people could not communicate with the

common Pidgin English or the official English language. Sometimes when Musa visited Onyekachi, they discussed other topics too, such as academics. Coupled with his interaction with other people, Onyekachi was learning the language quickly.

To reciprocate the gestures shown by Musa, one day Onyekachi decided to pay Musa a surprise visit—it would be his first time he'd gone there. He did not know that he was in for a huge embarrassment. As he entered the compound of the big fenced house, he found himself in a harem. At first, the women stared at him in shock. They had what looked like sacrilegious expressions written all over their faces. Every other thing that followed thereafter was not what he would consider as pleasant to remember. Whatever embarrassment he felt, however, was minor because he was not a full-grown man. He was to learn later that men, particularly strangers, were not allowed that kind of entry into such Muslim homes. It was a rule. He also learned that Musa's father, who was an Alhaji, was married to four women and had grown-up girls who also lived in the big fenced house. It was difficult for one to know because the women came out mostly in the dark of the night, still veiled. *Caged life!* Onyekachi had thought in his boyish mind. As he grew older, he would learn to respect and not criticize other religions and cultures.

Onyekachi explained to Nneoma that his embarrassment was worse because he could not speak Hausa and did not look like a Hausa. His height didn't help matters either, as they felt he was old enough to know of such rule and deliberately decided to flaunt it. Again, the inscription BA SHIGA, meaning No Entry, was boldly written on the door to the entrance of the big house, which was enough warning. But how could Onyekachi understand written Hausa when he could not even speak the language yet? His relationship with Musa ended after the incident.

The story had interested Nneoma, as she wondered how religion and culture differed in various places. Such an incident could not have happened in the East. More importantly, the East was not known for fanaticism and religious intolerance, which occasionally gingered up religious riots, looting, and killing that claimed thousands of lives. Onyekachi's father was a victim. But Nneoma longed to associate with people from other tribes, cultures, and religions. She loved to explore and wished to have Onyekachi's experience. Yet she had also resolved to remain at home if it would mean putting her life in jeopardy.

After his story, Nneoma had jokingly assured Onyekachi that nobody would embarrass him when she was around. She said that she would personally see to that by making sure she was always around him in school. So why abandon him in the classroom? Onyekachi wished that classes would commence immediately. He wanted attention to be shifted away from him, as he could hardly turn his head without catching somebody staring at him like he was Alice in Wonderland.

"Hey! *Nne*, take it easy. There's no prefect around to catch you," somebody said in a loud voice upon sighting Nneoma. She was sneaking into the class in a hurry.

"Latecomer Nneoma."

"Queen of all latecomers."

"Always late."

Comments were here and there in reaction to Nneoma's habit of being late. They weren't unusual, and Nneoma was used to their teasing.

"Ehenn? And who among you has not been late to school before?" Nneoma asked, jokingly.

"Me!" a student replied immediately, hand already raised as if waiting for the question.

"But your being late is something else!" another student exclaimed. He was sitting close to Onyekachi, who was relieved that Nneoma had arrived.

"Yes, you're right," yet another student added. "The only day she came to school on time was the day her cock laid an egg!"

There was an outburst of laughter in the class and even more laughter afterward as others said things to amuse the rest. It generated more noise in the classroom.

The classroom adjacent to JS2A was JS3C, which was a senior class. There was a particular student called Koyo in JS3C. Koyo liked to display his seniority to the lower classes, even when the occasion did not call for it. His arrogant nature had earned him much disrespect and contempt from students in the lower classes. Worse still, Koyo was neither a school functionary nor a bright student. Koyo was the first to react to the noise. He carried with him a long cane and moved into JS2A.

"Will you stop making noise?" Koyo ordered. "I warn you, if you make noise again this morning, I will flog all of you."

Nneoma, who was seated, got up slowly. In a contemptuous manner that she could not suppress, she regarded Koyo. "But we were only making *a noise* ... not *noise*."

Nneoma had hardly finished responding when nearly the entire class burst into laughter, which meant that they understood the correction she made which was meant to expose Koyo's poor English and humiliate him for his excessiveness.

Totally embarrassed and not in the shape to compete with Nneoma in the English language, Koyo snarled at her. "This girl ... You always challenge me in this school, eh?"

The laughter was amplified as Koyo, in a scurrying movement to leave the classroom, collided with the social studies teacher, who was coming into the classroom. She was also hurrying, as she was already fifteen minutes late and wouldn't want the principal to catch a glimpse of her.

"Oh! Sorry, sir," Koyo said, halting briefly.

"Oh! Sorry, 'miss,'" the teacher replied.

The laughter was endless as Koyo finally left, his head dropped in shame.

"Will you stop that?" ordered Miss Daniels, the social studies teacher.

The class quieted, and the laughter faded away.

Onyekachi was amused with the little scene.

Chapter 3

Two weeks had passed. Onyekachi was beginning to interact well with others and was getting familiar with the new school. He became acquainted with others as well. Without the help of Nneoma, the progress would not have been that fast.

"This is my brother, Kachi," said Nneoma, introducing Onyekachi to her friend. Although they were not biologically brother and sister, she was in the habit of referring to Onyekachi as her brother. Two things prompted this: the intimacy between them since their childhood and the common ancestry they shared, being from the same village.

"Kachi, this is my friend," Nneoma continued, touching the girl on her right shoulder with her left hand. "Her name is Njideka. She is my best friend."

"It's a pleasure meeting you," Onyekachi said, extending a hand toward Njideka. He tried to play "the man" by doing so, even though it was not in him. The only way to overcome that inherent thing in him was to take first action toward Njideka in the course of introduction. Speaking up first and extending a hand to her were the primary tricks needed.

Njideka took his hand—as if expecting it—and replied, "Thank you. It is my pleasure meeting you too."

Nneoma watched with interest as the boy and girl shook hands.

The trio, Nneoma, Njideka, and Onyekachi, formed a group among other groups of boys and girls emerging from the school gate after the short dismissal assembly. It appeared as if every student had a group that he or she was always attached to when they headed home after dismissal. It happened during breaks sometimes as well. The most common of the groups were those in twos. Very few students were seen walking home on their own, not attached to any group. Perhaps Onyekachi would have been seen among those if Nneoma was not in the school.

Previously, Nneoma and Njideka had passed the same road together after dismissal as a group of two. In the course of the journey home, Nneoma would eventually branch off to her house, relieve herself of the stuff she carried, and then see Njideka off. Njideka's house was farther away, in another village. It happened almost on a regular basis, except for days that either of them missed school. If it happened that Nneoma was absent, Njideka would stop in on her way home to find out what had hindered her from coming to school.

The practice of going home together after school was not the same when coming to school in the morning. Although her village was farther from the school, Njideka was usually the first student to get to school in the morning. There were occasions when she tried waiting for Nneoma so they could go together, but she ended up being late as well. Njideka therefore stopped waiting for Nneoma in the morning, for she hated to be punished or embarrassed about something that could be avoided. She was always punctual, in stark contrast to Nneoma's being late.

Turning toward Nneoma, who was in the middle, Njideka asked, "Is he that brother of yours you told me about who stays in the North?"

"Yes, you are correct, Njide," Nneoma replied. "He's the one I always tell you about. You remember my telling you too that I would tell his mother to bring him back home?"

Njideka looked out, not focusing on anything in particular, trying to recall. Nneoma had mentioned a village brother to her repeatedly, but she hadn't taken much interest and had never bothered to commit the details to memory.

"He left us," Nneoma continued, "after the third term of primary three to continue his education at Kaduna. His father took him away from me."

"From you? What do you mean?" Njideka was a little confused.

"Yes! Ask him. He knows what I mean very well. Let him explain everything himself."

Onyekachi was smiling. Nneoma was smiling too.

"Ah! I am lost. Is there anything that brother and sister are hiding from me?" asked Njideka jokingly.

"My dear, nobody is hiding anything from you. I wish he would come out of his shell and explain things himself ... and be part of this conversation." Nneoma said. Njideka was already beginning to observe that Onyekachi was not active in the conversation in which Nneoma intended him to play the lead role.

"Ha ... I am still lost here," Njideka persisted.

Just because Onyekachi had been schooling in the North didn't mean that he hadn't been visiting home. For about four years, he'd lived in the North, and some of his long vacations were spent at home. Nneoma, in her usual characteristic way, was always around to make them enjoyable for him. During the last long vacation before his transfer to the home school, Nneoma had told him so much about Njideka, extolling her virtues. In a bid to get Onyekachi acquainted with her, she planned for both of them to visit Njideka. The visit, an unscheduled one, was on a Sunday afternoon. Unfortunately, the day of the visit coincided with the day Njideka's father took her to Onitsha, after she had already spent part of her vacation at home. That day, Nneoma felt dejected. Whether it was a short or long vacation, Njideka had always spent part or all of it in Onitsha because her father wanted her to. She seemed to be her father's favorite child. Onyekachi was impressed with the kind of friendship between Nneoma and Njideka, and he wished to see her.

It was the first day of meeting Njideka since school had reopened. She could not start in the first or second week of reopening because her father wanted her to complete the private lessons she'd enrolled in in Onitsha during the vacation. It had always been the case with her father. He was convinced that the lessons were qualitative, hence he mandated her to complete them before returning home for school. He always wanted the best for her.

Both Onyekachi and Nneoma had been waiting for Njideka to return from Onitsha, and finally, she was with them. Nneoma could not conceal her excitement.

"God bless my soul!" she exclaimed. "I could not have wished for a better day, and the fun will not be complete if my brother is bent on making it appear like he's hiding something from Njide. So tell her ... Tell us!"

As they were walking down the road, they came to Onyekachi's magnificent house, which his late father had built. Onyekachi was already thinking of how to initiate breaking apart from the girls when he got to the gate. But Nneoma was quick to guess what was going through his mind.

"Kachi, now listen," Nneoma started again. "There is a tradition here that you must adhere to. It has to do with the daily seeing off of Njide, no matter how tight the situation. If you like, call it my personal tradition or whatever, but since it concerns you and me, and you are now part of us, you can't ignore it. It has automatically become your tradition too." She pointed at the gate and continued. "You must not abandon us there, unless you simply want to quickly enter the house to drop your things and rejoin us. When it is my turn, I will do the same too." She continued pointing at the gate and chuckled as if sounding a note of warning. Yet she was not done: "And remember, our conversation continues. Don't forget that you must give the details to Njide—about what really happened, and why I was angry that your father took you away from me."

Nneoma would always have her way. She knew how to cleverly approach issues and relate to situations to her own advantage. Onyekachi understood too. He knew her well enough. He knew also that her intention in trying to involve him to speak for himself was a calculated attempt to acquaint him with Njideka and remove all his shyness toward her.

He thought he had done his part already—he did not wait for Njideka to talk to him first after the introduction was made. He liked the courage with which she'd taken his hand. He knew what village girls were like. Their attitude toward boys, particularly city boys, depicted shyness or nervousness. Some people chose to refer to them as pretenders that often did the worst things when it had to do with morality and sexuality. Yet many others were of the opinion that village girls were decent, humble, and respectful. They were considered better choices for marriage to young men. They said city girls were exposed to all sorts of immoral acts, resulting in questionable moral standards. They were often accused of dressing provocatively. Most of them were seen lacking good home training and weren't humble and submissive to their husbands. Some of those attitudes were displayed under the aegis of civilization.

Unlike most village girls, city girls were full of self-confidence and composure. But it would be wrong to think of Njideka as a village girl. From what Nneoma had told Onyekachi about her, it meant that she only stayed in the village during school sessions.

He was happy he'd broken the ice with Njideka. But hadn't he done enough? How could Nneoma expect him to start telling his past childhood experiences to a stranger? But was she really a stranger? Something kept telling him that she was not, even though they'd just met for the first time. Her composure and smiles all depicted friendliness. She appeared unruffled, more unruffled than himself. Was she trying to intimidate him? No, he thought she was being natural. Yes, that was the word! He liked her for that.

"Nneoma, stop coaxing your brother to say what he is not in the mood to say. Maybe he needs some time to prepare himself to talk if it really mattered. I think he is doing the right thing in every way." Njideka came to Onyekachi's defense as if she were reading what was going through his mind.

Onyekachi noticed the use of the phrase "your brother" instead of "Kachi," which Nneoma had also mentioned to her.

"No … Njide. You are no other person," Nneoma grumbled, "and I'm sure he knows that well enough. If he is pulling my leg by choosing to remain silent on this one, I promise him I will not fall. He'd better give us the gist. Perhaps that would also bring his mind fully back to the good old days. Don't mind him; he can explain things well." Nneoma was adamant.

"But …"

"No buts, Njide. It's my case, and I'll handle it."

Onyekachi had always admired Nneoma for her willing spirit and resoluteness, but she could be stubborn sometimes. Was she not going too far? Again for all explanations, why would Nneoma want him to tell Njideka that she wanted him at home instead of relocating to Kaduna as that would have given her an opportunity of beating him in the class the second time? But he had to prove that his being silent on the topic in the presence of Njideka was not his weakness, lest she think that he was shy with her.

"Kachi, we're still waiting for you," Nneoma pressed.

"Okay, I'll tell her," he said. "I'll tell Njide."

Chapter 4

It was one of those Saturdays, in the month of April, characterized by heavy farming activities. On the weekends, students usually helped their parents do some farming work. Mrs. Ezinne Ikem preferred to hire hands to do her farming. Depending on what the hirer wanted done, there were two types of hired labor: one in which wage was paid and the laborer was fed, and the other in which it was wage only. In the former instance, depending on quality of work, the laborer was usually paid a fixed daily rate, while in the latter case, there was an agreement between the hirer and the laborer to do a particular farm job for a specified amount of money within a certain period. The latter types of hired labor apparently attracted higher wages than the former.

Mrs. Ikem preferred not to cook for laborers because the youngest of her female children, who was also her last child, was not at home to help with the cooking and other domestic chores. In a family of five children, Carol, eleven, was regarded as the baby of the house and would be expected to be at home with her mother as her helper. But Eze, the eldest son of the family, took her along with him to Kaduna shortly after the death of their father. Olachi was the first daughter, and next to Eze in age, but she lived in Lagos with Auntie Kate, while

Grace was at Port Harcourt with Uncle Sam. The difference between the ages of Olachi and Grace was about four and a half years.

Her health would only allow Mrs. Ikem to be involved in lighter farming activities, which it wasn't yet time for. Eze, who had been catering to the family's needs, had warned her to keep away from heavy activities to avoid jeopardizing her health. It was for that reason that she was at home on this typical Saturday morning. Since the death of her husband, Eze had been living up to expectations in the business he'd started in electronics sales.

Onyekachi was at home with his mother, making *ukwa,* a meal prepared from African breadfruit seeds, for lunch. Ukwa was a delicacy that took about three hours or more to prepare. It had to pass through different stages of preparation before it would be ready. The stages included heating the seeds, spreading and drying, threshing with pressure exerted through a cylindrical bottle, blowing off seed coverings, and handpicking to separate stuck seed coverings. It was finally washed and cooked. Cooking ukwa did not require a lot of cooking ingredients or spices since ukwa was naturally endowed with some of those. Ukwa was known for its high protein content.

During the handpicking stage, Mrs. Ikem and Onyekachi were joined by Uncle Eva's children. Uncle Eva was the youngest brother of Onyekachi's father. He was based at the village. Chudi, age eight, was in primary three; Harry, six, was in primary one; while little Lillian was in the nursery. On smaller trays, each of the kids had his or her own portion to pick. Mrs. Ikem and Oyekachi were doing theirs on bigger trays.

"Mama, how much do you like designing as a profession?" Onyekachi asked. Even when he was younger, he had always been enthusiastic about discussing with his mother, or anybody who cared to listen, what he would like to be in the future. He wanted input from his mother.

"Would that mean art design or engineering, or something like it?" asked Mrs. Ikem.

"Yes!" Onyekachi replied emphatically. "Engineering. My teacher told me that I must take science subjects in my senior secondary to keep the dream alive."

"I think I'd love that," said Mrs. Ikem. "You know, science and technology have done a lot of things in this world. The superpowers of the world have advanced tremendously in science and technology, and that is why they are ruling the world."

"I think I would prefer the area of engineering that deals with the design and construction of bridges and skyscrapers. Bridges like the Third Mainland Bridge and so on, the types I saw when I visited Auntie Kate in Lagos."

"That would be civil engineering, then," Mrs. Ikem concluded.

"Yes, Mama. That is exactly what I have in mind," Onyekachi confirmed. "Mama, the Third Mainland Bridge is so long that I wondered if there could be any other bridge longer than it in the whole world. The ingenuity of the engineers that designed and built it is something to reckon with."

"A lot of financial resources were spent in developing Lagos as Nigeria's former capital city to bring it to the state it is now, before the capital city status was finally moved to Abuja," Mrs. Ikem said.

"But, Mama, there's something that people who haven't been to Lagos may not know. They seem to think that everything about Lagos is paradise. It is not so at all! Many people in Lagos are living in slums too. In fact, a good number of people from this village who would come home during seasonal times to brag about Lagos actually live in such areas. During my stay, I had an opportunity to visit a particular area called Ajegunle. People also called it 'AJ City,' and this name sounds like it was such a nice place to be. But this is not true!" Onyekachi wrinkled his nose as he recalled the poor refuse and sewage state of the place. "The place was a mess!" he continued. "The kind of stench coming out from the static gutters in the streets was something I had not perceived in my life. There was scattered refuse and no proper dumping method. The whole place was so polluted that I wondered how the people adapted to that kind of poor environmental condition. Come to think of it, that area is only one of such areas in Lagos. It's common to have a family or group of four, five, or even six people sleeping in a single room. It is horrible."

"Yes," Mrs. Ikem confirmed. "One of the major problems with Lagos is population explosion. The population is much greater than what it should have been. You know, people are more attracted to the bigger cities than the smaller cities. Again, the poor state of things wouldn't have been this bad generally if not for the corruption that has plagued our nation for a long time. Most of our leaders are not sincerely concerned about the people's welfare."

"Well, I thank God for the area Auntie Kate lives in in Lagos," Onyekachi said. "She now lives on Victoria Island. The place is decent and beautiful, and I had a swell time during that holiday."

Auntie Kate was Mrs. Ikem's youngest sister. Her husband worked with a federal agency in Lagos. She was into supplying fabric materials to various offices, and she operated a variety store as well. She lived with Onyekachi's eldest sister, Olachi. After her marriage, Auntie Kate went five years without bearing children. Although her husband loved her, there was pressure on him by his relatives to end the marriage, but he did not give in. From those relatives, she suffered unbearable taunts associated with childlessness. They regarded her as a barren woman who would never conceive. They used all sorts of bitter and abusive language to frustrate her out of the marriage, including calling her a "male friend of her husband." Her husband had stood by her side and encouraged her. He had never ceased to use the words "God's time is the best" to her. When she was feeling depressed she pleaded to Mrs. Ikem and her husband to allow Olachi to live with her and her husband. It didn't take long after Olachi arrived for her to conceive. In a space of five years, she had a boy and two girls. She regarded the coming of Olachi to live with her as a blessing. She would do anything for her, as she would for her own children.

For the past six years that Olachi had been living in Lagos with Auntie Kate, she periodically visited her parents. She was multilingual. She wanted to marry a Yoruba man, but Mrs. Ikem objected. Mrs. Ikem wanted Olachi to finish her university education before marriage. She was not keen on the idea that her first daughter was considering marrying a man whom she regarded as from a distant land. That was barely a year after Mr. Ezekiel Ikem's death.

While Onyekachi engaged in conversation with his mother, the kids seemed not to be interested, probably because it was not within their understanding. As if to engage themselves in conversation too, the eldest of the three, Chudi, started up something.

"Did you remember what you dreamed last night?" Chudi asked inquiringly, specifically referring to Harry, his younger brother. Chudi was always telling his dreams to Harry.

"I dreamed a lot last night but I can't recall any of them now," Harry replied.

"I had one last night that was exciting and also scary," Chudi said.

Harry was clearly interested in hearing Chudi tell his dream. He adjusted his sitting position by stretching out his legs to relax properly.

Chudi also sat up from leaning against the wall to communicate better with his younger brother. Lillian was the only one who seemed not interested in any of the conversations.

"There were three witches chasing us—Chudi, Harry, Lillian, Mummy, and Daddy," Chudi began. "I was so fast, and I jumped into my car and zoomed off! The witches were fast too and began chasing after us in their own car."

"But you don't know how to drive," Harry reminded him.

"Remember that it was only a dream, and anything can happen in dreams," Chudi replied cleverly.

"But Mummy said that only people with fever have that kind of—"

"No!" Chudi interrupted. "You misunderstood Mummy. You don't have fever in all cases when you dream of driving or flying. Touch me." He took Harry's hand and pressed the back of it between his neck and chin. "Is my body hot?"

Since he was the older of the two, Chudi had a way of convincing his younger brother to agree with him. In one-on-one conversations with Harry, he also tended to say "Harry" instead of "you" when referring to his younger brother, and he said "Chudi" instead of "me" when referencing himself.

He continued. "In the next moment, Harry, Lillian, Mummy, and Daddy all started driving in their own cars, moving away from the witches. But Harry was not as fast as the others were."

The continuous mention of witches attracted the attention of Mrs. Ikem and Onyekachi, even though they'd pretended not to be listening.

"Suddenly, Harry was caught by the witches. Immediately, the leader of the witches brought out a long, sharp knife ..."

Harry winced.

"Shut up, Chudi," Mrs. Ikem interrupted. "Stop frightening the younger ones with that kind of gory story."

The reaction was instant, and Chudi immediately stopped, not concluding the story. The two boys concentrated more on doing their ukwa portions. From the different sizes of the ukwa portions the kids were doing, they were expected to finish in a common range of time. Lillian was the person with the smallest portion, yet it was likely that she would finish last.

"Brother Kachi, would you buy me a car?" Lillian asked.

For Onyekachi, it was an unexpected but not a surprising question. It was a typical kind of question from her. He thought for a while before he answered.

Onyekachi gave Lillian his adult-like assurance while patting her on the shoulder. "Yes, Lilly. I will buy a fine one for you, and not the type Chudi had in the land of the witches. Yours will be real and very nice."

"Are witches men or women?" Lillian asked, her inquisitive little mind wanting to know.

As Onyekachi sought the right answer to Lillian's second question, his mind was unable to concentrate because the recent mention of a car had rekindled his thoughts. What would the world be like when he became an accomplished civil engineer, owning a fleet of cars and magnificent buildings scattered across the country? That would be great! He was not just fantasizing; he believed. "After all, every achievement was once a dream!" he thought aloud.

Mrs. Ikem looked into his face, and Lillian also stared at him in surprise.

"Brother Kachi, did you dream too? You dreamed about achievement, didn't you?"

Chapter 5

On the surface, one might think that it was just a mere friendly atmosphere between the trio of Onyekachi, Nneoma, and Njideka. But on closer observation, it was much more than that. For Onyekachi and Nneoma, the bond between them was like that of a brother and a sister, even though they were not of the same parents. Since they'd grown to understand each other better, Onyekachi would never do anything to hurt Nneoma, at least not deliberately.

Even when they were much younger, the affection had been there. As far back as they could remember, Onyekachi would cuddle Nneoma to console her whenever she was upset or crying. He was sort of playing a big-brother role to her, despite the fact that they were age-mates. He made sure he protected her from other children who would cause trouble or pain to her. That Onyekachi never cuddled Nneoma anymore due to adolescent behavioral changes did not mean that his affection for her had diminished. Nneoma was the only girl with whom Onyekachi had not shown any tendencies toward shyness. And Nneoma had taken to Onyekachi like a biological brother, especially since she had none.

As for Nneoma and Njideka, they had known each other since they were in primary six. They first met in a quiz competition, representing their respective schools. They did exceptionally well whenever they represented their schools in such events. They became friends when their schools tied in one of those competitions. Therefore, it was a lovely coincidence for them to be posted to the same secondary school after their Common Entrance Examination. They had been close friends ever since. Apart from the academic bond between the girls, they had individual strengths which made up for each other's weaknesses in certain aspects of life. Among the qualities that Nneoma admired so much in Njideka was her discipline.

After their promotional examination to JS3, Onyekachi retained the same A class with Nneoma, but Njideka was swapped to B class in a random selection. Onyekachi's academic prowess and popularity with the school authority earned him a position as one of the school functionaries. It was unusual seeing that he had barely completed one full academic term when students in his class were made school functionaries.

Weeks had trickled into months since Onyekachi was first introduced to Njideka. On their first meeting, he did not feel anything special. But as time passed, and with the three coming together regularly, he started to develop something deep and strong for her in his heart. It was quite different from what he felt for Nneoma. Initially, it started as ordinary liking and then underwent some kind of change. Sometimes he could not hold back and did some silly things that surprised even himself. That had not happened to him before, and to think that sometimes he had no control over the feeling made it even stranger.

One day a boy named Goddy, who was also known as "The Bully," hit Njideka. He was bigger and older than any other member of JS3. Students had lost count of the number of times he was punished or suspended from school. Without his parents' influence, he would have been expelled a long time ago. Goddy carried himself in a manner reflective of ego and intimidation of others. He incessantly left his seat to occupy other students' seats, an attitude directed more to the girls.

The time came when Njideka's stool was the one Goddy opted for in the classroom. It happened repeatedly, until Njideka lost her usual patience and politeness and one day asked Goddy to vacate her stool for his. She used blunt words to tell him that she would not tolerate the inconveniencies anymore and demanded that he remained on his own stool. Insulted, the grumpy Goddy slapped Njideka across the face. The action resulted in an uproar, mainly among the female students in the classroom. Students in the adjoining JS3A were attracted by the noise. Some of them, including Onyekachi, moved closer to find out what was happening. On entering the classroom, Onyekachi noticed that Njideka's eyes were red and swollen. Immediately, he knew who the oppressor was, as he was already aware of the trouble that Goddy had been causing her. He cursed under his breath, and with a terrific impulse, he charged toward Goddy, giving him the blows of his life, with little or no chance to retaliate.

After meeting with the disciplinarian, it was obvious that Goddy was guilty and in need of punishment. Onyekachi was equally guilty for unwarranted interference. They were eventually taken to an old volleyball field that was overgrown with grass, where the disciplinarian marked out huge portions for them to cut. Had the principal been in school that day, they would also have been suspended from school for at least two weeks—in addition to grass cutting. That also would have culminated in their coming back from suspension with a written undertaking—a device of the principal.

While Goddy and Onyekachi were cutting grass on the pitch, Njideka sneaked out of the classroom to help Onyekachi. Nneoma also joined during break. Their combined effort made them finish the same day, leaving Goddy on the field to battle with his for two days. After the incident, Goddy never meddled in Njideka's affairs again.

Njideka fell ill and was taken to her father at Onitsha to be treated. The first day of her absence was somewhat bearable for Onyekachi, as he thought she would come to school the following day. He did not know that she was actually taken to Onitsha. So when a message got to him and Nneoma that Njideka's condition was rather serious, and that she might stay for some time in Onitsha to recover, it became unbearable for him. Each passing day seemed endless for Onyekachi as he prayed in earnest for Njideka to recover and come back to school. He was unable to concentrate during classes, and the harder he tried, the more difficult it became. His unusual quietness in the classroom became obvious to his classmates, who were quick to guess his predicament, as they all knew of his relationship with Njideka. Before long, Onyekachi also took ill.

"This is called 'sickness of no medication,'" someone in the classroom teased.

"Or you may want to call it 'sickness by induction,'" another student added.

The following morning, Njideka resumed school. She was so eager to see Onyekachi, but he was nowhere to be found. He was not at the assembly ground, where she had expected to meet him. Nneoma had not yet arrived, and she did not like asking other students about Onyekachi and Nneoma.

Since they had been promoted to the new class, Nneoma had tremendously improved in punctuality to school. It was largely the outcome of the responsibility passed to her by making her the school assembly prefect. It was an irony of purpose. Mr. Uche Dibia was well informed about Nneoma's tardiness habit, yet he decided to give her the post. He knew very well that she was among the brightest, and in his own typical way of building and developing young minds in all areas of academic excellence and character, he decided on the post for her. He believed that the sense of responsibility would compel her to change.

As an assembly prefect, Nneoma became the facilitator of all school assemblies and therefore was expected to come to school early every day. A roster was usually prepared by the assembly prefect, sharing the conduct of morning assemblies among the school functionaries and other willing members of the senior class. By doing so, the school aimed at making the students develop confidence and communication skills before any gathering, which would help equip them in leadership roles. In the event a student assigned to conduct did not show up, as was expected, the assembly prefect would take over. The assembly prefect was also expected to assist the student assigned to conduct assembly. Out of anxiety of facing the assembly, some students dodged the assignment with excuses like being sick or being late to school. Some even avoided coming to school entirely during their turn.

"*Chi mu o*, oh my God, the principal has finished me," Nneoma muttered the day she was announced as the assembly prefect. However, her father helped in waking her up on time.

"Nneoma, where's Kachi? Why didn't he come to school today? What happened to him?" Njideka asked impatiently. It was break period, and students were emerging from their classrooms.

"Njide, take it easy. First things first: how is your health now?"

"I'm fine now. But why didn't Kachi come to school today?" Njideka persisted.

"I can now understand that this husband of yours is very important to you," Nneoma joked. "He fell sick last week, and Mama suspects malaria. I was late to school this morning because I had to help Mama attend to him after attending to my father." Nneoma was trying to excuse herself for coming late to school that morning. She had earlier informed her assistant to take charge of the assembly that morning.

"Now can we go and see him?"

"Fine. You only have to wait for me under that mango tree." She pointed to a mango tree that provided shade. "I need to quickly go back to the classroom to lock my locker, and then I'll meet you there."

"It's okay by me, but make it snappy, please."

Nneoma ran off to the classroom, and upon getting to the door, she nearly collided with another female student who was also leaving the classroom in haste. The student gasped at the near miss and looked around to see if somebody was chasing Nneoma.

"What's chasing you?" the student asked.

"I think I should also ask you the same question," Nneoma replied.

The two girls finally smiled and went their separate ways.

Nneoma returned to meet Njideka under the mango tree, bringing some bananas and groundnuts for Onyekachi.

"Njide, let's be going. I'm ready."

"Ah! Did you move with jet speed?"

Mrs. Ikem was sitting in an armchair on the veranda in front of the house. She was studying the Bible with her prescription glasses, which she used whenever she read or wrote. Her posture and her glasses reminded one of a retired headmistress enjoying reading for pleasure. On seeing Nneoma and Njideka enter the compound, she removed her glasses to have a clearer view of the girls, which indicated that the glasses were used for reading and writing only. She beamed. She was actually surprised to see Njideka.

"Good day, Ma," the girls said simultaneously, bending their knees as a gesture of respect.

"Good day, my daughters," Mrs. Ikem responded. "Njideka, I was told you were sick too."

"Yes, Ma, but I am well now."

"I thought you had transferred to Onitsha."

"No. I hadn't the intention to transfer to Onitsha. I only went to receive treatment. I don't think I've had enough of your motherliness yet."

Mrs. Ikem admired the way Njideka related to make one feel important. On different encounters with her, she found her to be intelligent, polite, and full of respect for elderly people.

"He fell sick," said Mrs. Ikem, shifting the topic and knowing why the girls had come. "He's having chills and fever. Occasionally, he develops malaria bouts, and our family doctor suggested that I treat him with chloroquine and paracetamol, to go along with phenergan. The phenergan will keep the chloroquine from itching him since he is allergic to chloroquine." Mrs. Ikem spent a little time explaining to the girls, lest they began to think she practiced self-medication as some local people did.

"I do understand," she continued, "that phenergan also causes drowsiness, but nevertheless, you girls can go in and see him."

"Thank you, Ma," the girls responded.

They moved through the corridor and into Onyekachi's room. Onyekachi was fast asleep when they entered. Njideka felt his body temperature and watched him closely and affectionately while Nneoma looked on. Noticing that Onyekachi was unlikely to wake up soon from the deep sleep, Nneoma took the bananas and groundnuts that Njideka had earlier dropped on Onyekachi's reading table, placing them on a stool by the side of his bed. While Njideka was contemplating waking him up, Nneoma cut her short.

"Dr. Njideka, the bell has rung. Break is over."

Chapter 6

Njideka was not the first child in her immediate family, but she commanded more respect from her parents than any of her sisters did. In a family of three girls and two boys, Njideka was the third child and the third daughter as well. The two boys were a set of twins. Her two elder sisters, Lucy and Celia, had always regarded their parents' attitude, especially their mother's, as unfair. They compared the kind of treatment Njideka got with how they were treated. On certain occasions, they confronted their mother and would have done the same to their father had their courage not failed them.

"Mama, we want to know why you're always harsh on us," inquired Celia, the younger of the two sisters. Celia was two years younger than Lucy was, but Celia was taller and bigger. If the two girls were placed side by side, it would take the instinct and eye of a mature person to observe that Lucy was older. To make it even more difficult for any outsider to appreciate the fact, Celia overshadowed Lucy in so many things.

"I don't understand, my daughter. What do you mean?" replied Ego, their mother.

"Mama, she means that you don't give us a free hand as you usually do with Njideka, our kid sister," Lucy quickly intervened,

41

suggesting that their mother didn't always give them freedom as they required.

"I still don't understand. What do you mean by 'a free hand'?" Ego knew where they were heading but pretended not to know. She wanted them to be more specific about what they meant before they retreated. She knew her onions as a good mother would.

Celia, who had been wanting to get their mother's full attention on the issue, cleared her throat in preparation to talk. There was cynicism in the throat clearing, as she believed that the reaction or response they would receive from their mother on the issue would not favor them.

"Mama, it still beats our imaginations that, as the eldest children of the family, we are not accorded our privileges at all," Celia started.

"What privileges have I deprived you, my daughters?"

"Why is it that whenever any person, particularly if he is a boy, comes around asking for Lucy or me, you place him under tough questioning? Why is it that we are hated? Why do you and Papa treat us like people who cannot distinguish between their right and left? The other day, our kid sister, Njideka, came home with her two friends, whom you welcomed. Another day the boy came alone to visit but there was no tough questioning for him. Instead, you asked about his parents and siblings as if he were a relative. It still beats our imaginations that at our age, you treat us like kids in anything pertaining to boy-girl relationships when compared to Njideka. Is that not favoritism?"

Lucy was nodding in approval to the barrage of questions and complaints channeled toward their mother on their behalf. But Ego would not be conned into believing them.

"Have any of the boys who came looking for any of you—even in your blindness—appeared or behaved like people who have good home training? Have they ever behaved like decent people from responsible homes? Have you girls ever paused to consider the reputation this family enjoys … and how it can be marred with unwholesome relationships with boys?" It was typical of Ego to use hard, persuasive questions when dealing with people. She applied it to her children too whenever it mattered. She was not done yet.

"Now, I want you girls to listen carefully: nobody—I repeat, *nobody*—is given a free hand to bring boyfriends in this house. You are only allowed to bring decent and good friends who have genuine intentions. Everybody must adhere to this. Every one of you must be responsible. Maturity is more of a thing of attitude—positive attitude—and not necessarily age, as you girls think most often. Mature children are responsible children, and responsible children are the pride of any parent. The truth is that what you prove yourself to be determines whether you get respect from people or not." She could go on and on with the sermon. After all, she was once a Sunday school teacher. She was so good with any issue that had to do with morals.

The two girls were dumbfounded at the end of their mother's speech on morals. They did not know what to say. They became unrepentantly ashamed when their mother talked about the issue of decency. This was because none of the boys who had visited them proved to be decent, at least in appearance and dressing. First impressions really mattered! They felt jealous pangs rise in them to observe that Njideka's friends—Onyekachi and Nneoma—painted the picture of the so-called decent people in their mother's calculation. They became more jealous of Njideka, as everything their mother said seemed to favor her, even though she was not with them when they confronted her. Feeling defeated for not being able to influence their mother, Celia and Lucy turned to leave. But when they were just a few paces away, their mother called out to them, and they turned.

"Girls, I don't hate you and never will. I love you all and always want the best from you. It is my duty as a mother to encourage you to achieve the best in life." Ego smiled to them as she said this.

As the girls entered the corridor of the house, which linked to different rooms, Njideka, who was pressing herself against a window in her room, eavesdropping on their conversation, quickly made a dash to her bed and lay in it. Facing the wall, she pretended to be asleep. She shared the room with one of her cousins, who was not around at the time. The girls moved into her room, and Celia quickly stepped toward the bed, tapping her hard on the shoulder.

"Njideka ... Njideka ... Come on—wake up!"

She pretended to be in deep sleep.

"Please mind how you touch her. You know she is an egg," Lucy mocked. "She might be rushed to Onitsha for proper medical treatment. Don't forget that she arrived just a few days back. Of course the local chemist is good enough for you and me!"

"I-I don't care ... Njideka! Njideka!" Celia tapped harder.

"Mmm ... mmm?" Njideka responded slowly.

"Where is the book you took from my room before you went to Onitsha?"

"Which book is that, please?" Njideka asked her in return, sitting up on the bed and rubbing her eyes.

"Good girl! You are asking me, eh? It's *Wedlock of the Gods*."

"Okay, I remember. One of my friends has it."

"What! One of your ... What does that mean? Please get it from him before I lose my temper."

"Sister Celia, please just give me until tomorrow. I promise I will get your book back from Nneoma. She must be through with it by now. It's not a 'him' who has your book as you're suggesting."

The following Tuesday morning, while Njideka was going to school, she was worried. The situation at her home made her sad. She could not understand why her elder sisters believed she was making them appear as the black sheep of the family and on the other hand making herself appear as the good girl before their parents. Any slight provocation on them at home would be a transferred aggression to her. What marveled her also was the speed with which her sisters would calm down immediately whenever such an incident occurred, thereafter behaving normally toward her. She knew that her sisters did not actually hate her.

She recalled an incident when a boy waylaid her on her way home from school ... and what followed thereafter. The boy had been chasing her, but she ignored him. In his frustration, the boy thought that the next line of action should be to beat the hell out of her for rejecting him. When she got home and told her sisters what had happened, and how a passerby intervened to stop the boy from attacking her, they were not satisfied. Anger surged through them. That protective and powerful love that bonded people from the same womb pushed them into their rooms to dress in shorts in readiness for a fight. They combed the village and later found the boy in the neighborhood. They beat him black and blue and left him with a memory of the bitter lesson. They acted like mad girls.

Because Njideka had just recovered from ill health, she was advised to take *okada*, a motorcycle, to school. An okada driver would pick her up. Although her elder sisters were happy that she had recovered, it did not stop them from believing that asking her to go to school by okada for the time being was overpampering. But Ego told them that it was at their father's request, and there must be a reason for that. She tried reassuring them once more that their minds as parents were not biased to the kind of treatment they gave them individually as their children. She went further, pointing out to them occasions when they were given special treatment when the circumstances called for such. In their haste to jump to conclusions, they'd forgotten too soon.

As Njideka sat on the passenger seat of the okada, with both legs to one side, she had already made up her mind to stop at Onyekachi's.

When Onyekachi woke up after the girls left yesterday, he saw the bananas and groundnuts on the stool by the side of his bed. He definitely knew that his mother couldn't have bought them. She preferred to buy foods like meat pie or boiled eggs instead of bananas. She seemed to agree with the opinion of some people that eating too many sugary things like bananas aided the activities of worms in the bowels.

Mrs. Ikem had told him that Njideka and Nneoma had brought the bananas and groundnuts, and that they decided not to wake him since he was in a deep sleep.

So she's back, Onyekachi thought. *Perhaps my spirit drew her back. But what would have been more soothing than being awakened from sleep by Njide?*

Mrs. Ikem had planned to take Onyekachi to the clinic for more treatment if symptoms persisted after the malaria dosage she'd administered to him. She was particularly worried that Onyekachi, who hardly ever rejected food, looked at food as a disgusting thing and made no effort to eat while on his sick bed. Last night, even after much persuasion, Onyekachi refused to have dinner. Breakfast was ready, but all he could do was stare at it from his bed. Mrs. Ikem also feared that he was losing more and more strength.

She had gone to arrange for a vehicle to take Onyekachi to the clinic by midday. No sooner had she gone in search of a vehicle than Njideka arrived. She alighted from the okada and handed over a ten-naira note, which she produced from the school bag she carried with her, to the okada man. The okada man stood astride on the motorcycle, dipped his left hand into his trouser pocket, and brought out crumpled naira notes. He singled out a five-naira note gave it to her as her change. Having done that, he revved the motorcycle and then sped off like an expert rider, the way okada men do to demonstrate their foolhardy skills. Njideka thanked God that she had already alighted, for she had heard stories about people who'd gone on okadas and were pulled to pieces in accidents before they reached their destinations. Some okada accidents had been associated with crashes with heavy vehicles like trucks and trailers. Most victims of accidents at the orthopedic hospitals were from okadas, as most okada drivers were very careless and never safety conscious.

When Njideka arrived and noticed that Mrs. Ikem was not around, she darted toward Onyekachi's room, and upon reaching the door, she knocked and entered without waiting for a response.

"What's the matter with you?" Njideka queried.

"How is your health now?" Onyekachi inquired.

"Don't bother yourself about my health; I should be asking you!" she said. Turning slightly, she saw the breakfast on the side stool. "That's your food, isn't it? Don't you feel like eating?"

"No ..."

"You can't say that, Kachi." She felt the food. "The *akamu* and *akara* are gradually getting cold, and we both know very well that they are better when warm."

"But, Njide, I have no appetite for them. Please take them on my behalf, if you like."

"You can't be serious! You must be kidding. Look, Kachi, stop this joke and eat your breakfast; you need strength!"

"But ..."

"No buts," she interrupted, "and let's not argue over this. Do you know that eating your food will give you strength?"

"Yes," he replied.

"And do you love me?" she asked him.

On his sick bed, Onyekachi became more alert. He'd never expected that question. Both of them had always expressed their feelings to each other through their actions but had not really spoken them aloud to each other.

"Yes, yes, I do," he answered, the words coming out spontaneously.

"If you do, then I should be able to persuade you to take the food whether you have an appetite for it or not," she said. "So please kindly sit up, and if you don't mind, I can feed you. I think you're weak."

Onyekachi sat up. Now more conscious of the realities of those words, he allowed Njideka to feed him. She sat closer to him and started feeding him the akamu and akara balls. Even when he was full, he didn't bother to tell her, for he wanted to prove to her how much he loved her. He kept taking more and more.

Then it happened without warning: he suddenly began to vomit what he had eaten, and some of it spattered on her school uniform. In amazement mixed with excitement, the boy and the girl looked each other straight in the eyes. And the boy asked her, "Do you love me?"

She nodded and replied, "Yes, of course!"

"Then find a place in your heart to forgive me for this," he said, pointing to the mess spattered on her uniform.

Chapter 7

Many people dreaded leap year. Popular opinion and belief, mostly from folks in the villages, associated each leap year with more deaths. It was likely that a curious student like Nneoma would want to inquire from her teachers what leap year and all the associated stories were about. As expected, she raised the question to their integrated science teacher as he rounded off a topic on energy. The teacher did not disappoint. He used the simplest scientific way to explain the leap year concept. Nneoma was delighted and determined to tell her father this when she got home. She was used to sharing the knowledge she acquired from school with her father, who had little formal education.

"Papa, what some people believe about leap year is superstition," Nneoma said. She was home from school and had changed out of her school clothes. She moved closer to Dee Nico, who was relaxing in an armchair under the tropical almond tree. The umbrella-like tree provided shade inside the compound. It was a sunny afternoon, and the rooms in the house were too hot for comfortable relaxation. He'd decided to stay outside and savor the gentle afternoon breeze under the shade trees, seeing as how he hadn't had much work that day and was home quite early. Nneoma sat on a small chair facing him.

"So how did you come about that conclusion, my daughter?" Dee Nico asked.

"It is a baseless and irrational belief," Nneoma said authoritatively. "In these modern times, anything that has no scientific proof should be discarded, and I think the earlier people realize this, the better for them."

"You still haven't answered my question." He was the type who liked to be convinced thoroughly by his opponent in any discussion or argument before conceding, particularly when he had contributions to make. He loved chatting with Nneoma so much, as he enjoyed her company. Since the death of Ure, Nneoma meant everything to him. He cherished the girl so much that he would do anything within his ability to make her happy. Some people, however, said that he overpampered her.

"Our integrated science teacher," Nneoma began, "was able to prove to us why there is leap year ... and what it's all about." She adjusted her sitting position and continued. "It might be a little difficult for you to understand, but I'll try. I'll begin by telling you that the earth is like a ball—*spherical* is the right English word. It makes constant movement around the sun, which takes a period of three hundred sixty-five and one-quarter days to complete a full cycle, and that makes a year in our calendar. But the quarter day is usually added up to one full day in four successive years. Subsequently, this additional one day in every four successive years is then added to the month of February to make the number of days twenty-nine instead of the usual twenty-eight. This makes the number of days in that particular fourth year three hundred and sixty-six instead of the normal three hundred and sixty-five days. When this happens, it becomes leap year, as it is now. And this also means that the next leap year will be in the next four years ... and so on."

With Dee Nico's lost look at Nneoma, it was clear that she had not communicated this well. She knew that most of the things she said sounded abstract to him, but she did not know any other means to use to deliver the message to make him understand. She believed she used the simplest language one could use to explain the subject. Dee Nico would have paused her if he weren't such a patient man. He was calm. He always gave his opponent time to air his or her views, and he expected that in return.

"You see, my daughter, inasmuch as I know that this science your teacher tells you about has done so many things, it's difficult to believe or even understand it. How do you expect me to believe that the world is like a football, yet we don't slip off it?"

"In science, there is a force called the force of gravity, and it prevents that," Nneoma explained.

Dee Nico shook his head, as Nneoma's attempt to explain further seemed to have complicated it. "So if the world is moving, why are we not feeling the movement? Even a baby in a moving vehicle understands that it is moving, so why can't we feel this movement? If it is moving like you said, why must it always be around the sun? And this force you're talking about, how does it work?"

Nneoma was sure that she had bitten off more than she could chew. How was she to explain all these things to her father, some of which she did not know in detail?

Dee Nico was determined to pass across his point of view on the subject to convince her of what he thought and believed. "You see, my daughter, there are so many questions without answers in science. I don't think that leap year is a science issue, even though it is the same white man who talks about science that gave it the name 'leap year,' and we adopted it. I don't really know, but I think the issue is with the name, which is the reason for so many cases of death. In our culture, a name helps determine a child's destiny, and it applies to other things as well. If you name a child *Omekagu*, he would start to act like a leopard beginning in his childhood to demonstrate his strength and invincibility even before he grows into a man. I think the name 'leap year' means 'death year.' It was in a leap year that my only and elder brother that my mother also gave birth to died when we were growing into manhood. It was in another leap year that my mother died—although your mother's, my wife's, own case was a little different. Still, it was ..." It became difficult for Dee Nico to finish.

"No, Papa. It was coincidence—sheer coincidence. Coincidence is a common thing in nature, and it happens everywhere in the world."

"Yes," Dee Nico said, still being calm, "I know that events coincide. Sometimes I ask myself too why the impact of leap year is more pronounced in our family. It is so difficult to understand. I always feel compelled to pray more during leap years than other years, like I am doing this year. Sometimes I get nervous about the unknown. I just think that we have to be more careful."

His deep words made Nneoma feel a chill run down her spine.

When he observed that Nneoma had kept silent for some time, which was most unusual, he knew immediately that something was wrong. Nneoma could not had been silent for that long on an issue for which she believed she had the trump card since it had science backing. Similarly, in the past, she would argue it to the last, using any conceivable point or fact to try convincing her father. In demonstration of maturity, Dee Nico would give in to avoid dragging it out for too long. Nneoma had never given in to any science-oriented argument in the past. Certainly, something was wrong, and Dee Nico knew it.

"*Nne m*, my sweetheart, what's the matter with you? You appear too quiet. I do hope that I have not frightened you in any way. There is nothing to worry about or be scared of; God cares," Dee Nico consoled. He touched her hand and gave her a tender squeeze. "Why not go and get lunch for us? Surely you must be hungry, for you've not had lunch since you arrived home from school."

Nneoma stood up from the chair and walked into the kitchen. She arranged some firewood under the tripod and poured a small amount of kerosene to the wood. She took a matchbox from the shelf, but opened it to find it empty. She hissed, dropped the matchbox, and moved into her room to fetch the one she kept by the window frame at the side of her bed. She usually kept one within easy reach in the event of an emergency in the night, as Dee Nico had taught her. The electric transformer for the village hadn't been functioning, and there had been no electricity lately. She lit the firewood and placed the pot of *jollof* rice on the tripod. When the food was warm and ready, she called out to her father.

"Papa, would you like to eat the food in your room?"

"Bring the food out here for us, my daughter. The rooms are too hot," Dee Nico replied.

About two weeks later, on a Friday, Dee Nico came back from his normal daily job earlier than usual. He'd felt sick at his workplace. He got in his favorite position under the almond tree, and after half an hour, he dozed off. Dee Nico was still asleep when the gigantic school bell for Umuagu Secondary School rang, signaling dismissal.

After the dismissal assembly which was usually brief, Nneoma proceeded home. Junior Secondary Certificate Examination, popularly known as Junior WAEC, would be starting by next term. To make students fully prepared for the examination, the school authority organized additional evening lessons. Umuagu Secondary School had a reputation for producing students who did exceptionally well in the external examination, which it wanted to maintain to keep its flag flying high in the state. Students whose homes were closer to the school usually went home after dismissal, only to join others later for the lessons. Though Oyekachi was among those, he stayed behind to keep Njideka company. She always stayed behind because her house was farther away. They usually bought snacks to appease hunger and got involved in academic chats. Nneoma would join later with a supply of fruits before lessons commenced.

Nneoma saw her father from a distance, under the almond tree in his favorite armchair. His head sloped backward as he rested his back on the support. She increased her pace and arrived at the compound.

"Papa! Papa, you are back from work quite early today. Did you do less work today?" There was no response from Dee Nico, nor did he move. Nneoma drew closer to him, placed her hand on his lap, and shook him enough to wake him. "Papa, is everything okay?"

"Is it you, my daughter?" Dee Nico responded. He opened his eyes slowly, not adjusting his position.

"Sit up, Papa, and talk to me. You look anxious. What is the matter?" Nneoma became worried.

"I have a headache; my head is throbbing."

"Okay, I'll get some tablets for you," Nneoma said, rushing into Dee Nico's room. She came out with two tablets of paracetamol and a cup of water. After Dee Nico had taken the tablets, Nneoma persuaded him to enter his room and lie down.

Dee Nico's condition improved, and Nneoma was happy with that. After having dinner with her father, Nneoma moved into her room to do an assignment on simultaneous equations. The assignment was given at the evening lesson, which she could not attend because she'd stayed to nurse her father. Onyekachi and Njideka had briefed her when they stopped by after the lessons.

There were five problems on the mathematics topic, and Nneoma had solved four, but the last one proved a hard nut to crack. She tried different approaches to solving the problem, to no avail. She finally retired to her bed, as it was getting late in the night. She was still wondering if there was anything she'd missed in her approaches, or whether the teacher had introduced another approach in her absence, which she could have used. As she was still trying to figure out in her head some other methods that might work, she drifted into sleep. A few hours later, from an impulsion she did not understand, she woke up instantly and moved into her father's room, lying in a smaller bed opposite her father's. She fell back asleep.

At about four in the morning, Dee Nico started to breathe heavily. The sound of his breathing was heavy enough to wake Nneoma, who was fast asleep. Dee Nico had never snored while he slept, but this was different. Startled, Nneoma got up from her bed and moved to the table where the burning lantern was kept underneath. She placed the lantern on the table and turned the wick up; the room became brighter. She moved toward her father, and observing his condition, she became more startled.

"Papa ... Papa, what is the matter with you?"

"My-my d-d-daughter," Dee Nico stammered with a husky voice, "my whole body is so h-e-e-a-vy."

Nneoma was confused about what to do or say. She became bereft of ideas. In seconds, it occurred to her that the situation required a more mature person to help. She immediately thought of her nearest next of kin living nearby, Uncle Jonah. Uncle Jonah was a half brother to Dee Nico, and his mother was the second wife of their late father. He'd used greed and threats to snatch some of the family lands and valuable trees. He stopped at nothing to get whatever he wanted. Nneoma had never liked him, but because of the situation at hand, she had to get him before things got worse. Nneoma did not fear the darkness as she ran to Uncle Jonah's house. In a few minutes, she returned with him, although he had shown initial reluctance to follow her.

"Nicodemus, what is the matter with you?" Uncle Jonah asked in a deep masculine voice.

Ple-please ta-take care of m-my daughter," Dee Nico managed to say. As if waiting for Uncle Jonah to come so that he could deliver the message, he took a deep, choking breath and breathed his last. Though she never wanted to accept it, nobody needed to tell Nneoma that she had been rendered a complete orphan with that breath.

Her wail tore into the darkness and woke some neighbors. In minutes, the compound was filled with men, mostly armed. It was still dark, and women seldom came out in such situations in case it turned out to be armed robbers or thieves attacking someone. The men, armed, would be equal to the task.

Nneoma thought about herself—no father, no mother, no brother, and no sister. She was officially an orphan. Who would sponsor her education; who would take care of her welfare and feeding? She thought about her father's caring nature. To her, her father doubled as both father and mother since she'd never known her mother. She'd never lacked anything with him. Those flashes crossed her mind.

She wept and wept and wept. Like Rachel in the Bible, who refused to be comforted because her children were no more, she also refused to be comforted. For the cold hands of death to snatch away her greatest treasure in a most mysterious way was the cruelest thing.

Perhaps somebody was up to mortal mischief, using leap year as camouflage.

Chapter 8

The trio of Onyekachi, Nneoma, and Njideka passed their JSCE very well. Their results were the best in Umuagu Secondary School. In a send-forth ceremony organized by the school, prizes were given to outstanding students.

After the death of her father, Uncle Jonah practically ignored everything about Nneoma's education. His interests were on the portions of land and economic trees that belonged to the late Dee Nico. Eleven months before the death of Dee Nico, land matters had generated serious disputes to the extent that the kindred elders had to intervene. An *Orie* market day, a local weekday, was scheduled to share the properties. But Uncle Jonah came up with a game plan that created confusion among the gathered elders, as most of them started arguing noisily about nonissues and dispersed angrily. He did not want the properties to be shared. It happened repeatedly, whenever there were such gatherings, until the day the elders became wiser and refused to be used or confused. They also refused to be intimidated from discharging their responsibilities. That fateful day was a different story for the antagonist, as his aims were defeated. The landed properties and economic trees were shared among the family members. Now, with Dee Nico dead, all he had was automatically transferred to Nneoma. It wouldn't have been difficult for Uncle

Jonah to snatch Nneoma's inheritance, but he knew that people were watching. He pretended to be uninterested so as not to raise any form of sneaking suspicion about him being responsible for the death of Dee Nico.

Anyway, the girl will get married, he said to himself. *She definitely won't remain in the family. It's just a matter of time—a little more time.*

Uncle Jonah acted like an evil genius. He silently became more aggressive to the poor girl. As expected of the next of kin to help her, he refused to render any form of help whatsoever. He used all kinds of tricks to try to persuade her to give up going to school, hiding under the pretence of "tough times."

"You are the daughter of my late brother, Nicodemus," Uncle Jonah said. "I want the best for you, just like my brother wanted when he was alive. May the good Lord grant him eternal rest. I think the best thing for you now is to start petty trading, getting some money to take care of yourself. Education for women ends in the kitchen. So why do you have to be going hungry to get education when you know that eventually you must end it all in a man's kitchen? As a petty trader, you make some money to maintain yourself, and any man who sees you will like and appreciate your beauty and hard work. You may be thinking that I don't contribute to your education—this is because I have too many expenses. So many things rest on my shoulders. My children are all in school and things are tough! I shall soon withdraw some of them."

Uncle Jonah was always quick to give a false impression of himself before the public, with claims of giving the poor girl all the necessary help she needed. Nneoma's maternal uncles and aunts were not helpful either. The only one who would have been in a better and willing position to help was the one who'd once lived with her husband in Enugu. She was her mother's elder sister. Her husband had since retired from active service from the National Railway Cooperation and had not received his retirement pay.

But in all these tribulations, Nneoma was undaunted in her quest for survival in life.

Before the death of her father, Nneoma had reiterated her position on becoming a nun. She wanted to dedicate herself to the service of God and humanity. Since some regarded her as a child of mystery, she had a conviction that the best way to make a difference in her life would be to serve God. It never bothered her since she too thought that God worked in mysterious ways. Being a nun would afford her the opportunity to be close to her father continually. Nneoma was bent on being a nun, and nothing would stop her. It was her greatest desire. Dee Nico had not objected to that.

"My daughter," Dee Nico had said, "it is a wonderful idea. I am willing and ready to support you in any vocation you have chosen. After all, your happiness is my happiness too. But I want to believe that you are fully aware of what it means and takes to become a reverend sister. One has to take a vow of poverty, chastity, and obedience. Again, one must have a calling from God."

Nneoma had replied, "I understand, Papa. But poverty, as it is said, does not mean that we won't be having our three square meals as usual . . . or have a decent life."

She had resolved that after JSCE, she would enroll in the nearest convent school in the area for her senior secondary education, from where she would go higher in her education and training for the final profession of vows. With Dee Nico dead and close relatives not supportive, the plan of enrolling in a convent after her JSCE turned bleak.

Out of compassion for Nneoma, Mrs. Ikem took up her sponsorship. She was ever impressed with the peculiar bond between Onyekachi and Nneoma. She was helping with the remaining portion of the allowance Eze usually sent. It would have been money that she would have saved. She would have enrolled Nneoma in the convent school immediately after JSCE except for the bigger financial involvement. Apart from the school fees, one had to pay for boarding accommodations and meals because such institutions only offered admission to boarding students.

Nevertheless, Mrs. Ikem assured Nneoma that credit passes in her SSCE result, including English language and mathematics, would garner support for her to enter a higher convent school. She had already begun making contact with the local priest who had shown willingness to assist.

"This could only be possible with a good result," Mrs. Ikem asserted.

"I promise. My result will be good when I write SSCE in three years' time," Nneoma said, her eyes filled with tears of joy and gratitude. "I am very grateful. You have always proved to be a mother to me, indeed. God will surely reward you."

"Get up, my daughter." Mrs. Ikem motioned with her hand. She stretched out her hand and helped her up from her kneeling position. "I have warned you several times to stop crying. *Oya*, now, take this handkerchief and dry those tears immediately!" Mrs. Ikem handed her a neat white handkerchief.

Comprehensive High School Nuso was a bigger secondary school than Umuagu Secondary School. Not only was it a combination of both junior and senior secondary, but the school had better structures. It wasn't a boarding school per se, but it did provide boarding facilities for a few students who came from distant places. They lived in a dormitory. The student population of CHSN—as it was popularly called—was more than three times that of Umuagu Secondary School. Considering its population, one would begin to imagine why the elderly principal of Umuagu Secondary School, Mr. Uche Dibia, who was close to retirement, preferred a school like Umuagu.

Onyekachi was in SSIA class, and Nneoma was in SSID class. CHSN was farther from home. They had to walk a long way to school every day, which meant that they had to leave home earlier. Nneoma had since dumped her habit of arriving late.

Nneoma was growing into a more beautiful girl. Some male students in higher SS classes could hardly keep their eyes off her. Some lustful teachers were not exonerated either! At senior secondary, it was common for boys to discuss their escapades with girls when they gathered. It was becoming rampant among those who weren't serious about their academics. Chasing girls had become important business, no longer just a pastime. Boys who were successful in chasing girls referred to themselves as "big boys." The activity was more at the beginning of new sessions as newcomers arrived at the schools. Some of the boys who considered themselves smart would make early "moves" on the new girls.

"*Bros, how e go be dis term?*" a tall boy asked his friend in Pidgin English, inquiring about the plan for the new session. The two boys were standing close to each other on the pavement in front of a classroom block.

"As in what?" the friend and the shorter of the two asked.

"*Nna a*, stop pretending as if you don't know what brought you to school this first week of reopen, or did you do exactly this way last term?" the taller boy said.

The shorter boy became more purposeful. "Okay ... okay, I'm only pulling your legs. So what's happening? You know, today is the fourth day since school reopened."

"I have just seen one babe. She's light in complexion. I think she's from Umuagu."

"Hey, guys, *which one una dey? How e go be?*" Another boy had joined them from behind, folding his arms around the other two boys' necks, one arm for each neck. Although his initial words were a greeting, his arrival was sudden and unannounced, making the other two nearly bolt, thinking that it was trouble.

"Stanley, my guy," the taller boy said as he turned his head, "you scared me to death the way you arrived. *How far?*"

"Since the first day that school reopened, I've been around," the boy addressed as Stanley replied. "I've done my homework very well this time, and all I can say now is that I'm ready for action."

"Have you seen any?" the taller boy asked.

"Yes, I have ... since the first day school reopened, when she started her registration process. Bright would know her since his village is closer to hers. But there is this guy that perches around the babe. I was taking him to be her boyfriend, but my investigations revealed that he is her brother. I also learned that she dumped her initial plan of becoming a reverend sister, and that puts her suitable for me. Of course, she wouldn't have wasted such beauty! I'll strike soon. I'm just waiting for her brother to give her a little breathing space so I can corner her. In short, the girl is already mine."

"Do you know her name and where she comes from?" the taller boy pressed on.

"My guy, I told you that I have done detailed investigations. Her name is Nneoma; she is from Umuagu Secondary School," Stanley added.

"Withdraw, Stanley. The babe is mine," the taller boy advised, or rather, he warned. "Withdraw before you spoil things for others."

"No, Charles. No! Is it because of the mistake I made last session while chasing the other babe? Then I thought I could use memorized words for that kind of business, but I forgot my line and the words stuck. Again, that was my first time. Nobody would say that he didn't make some kind of mistake doing something the very first time. There is always a first time ... or have you forgotten? Anyway, I've learned my lesson and have also taken correction. The girl is already mine," Stanley boasted.

The two boys started dragging out the issue, which gradually developed into a squabble. Charles, the tallest of the three, prided himself on being versatile and well experienced in activities involving chasing girls, and he considered Stanley an amateur or novice. Stanley did not like it, and he referred to Charles as *iti* since he knew he was better academically.

"Hey, guys, stop this! You're fighting over a girl who doesn't know you exist? That's funny! But, Charles, I think you should leave her for Stanley since you already got one last session. Many more babes are coming—more beautiful babes."

Bright finally settled the matter, even though Charles was not willing to give in to Stanley. Eventually, Stanley approached Nneoma, who turned him down in such a manner that his ego was terribly bruised.

After Stanley's nauseating approach, Nneoma thought that it was over, but little did she know that it was just the tip of the iceberg.

Mr. Uka taught English lit. Students nicknamed him "Demo," which stood for demonstration. He could demonstrate and gesture with any movable part of his body to drive home his points when teaching or talking. Mr. Uka was the form teacher of SSID class. He was in charge of the school library, where he had a separate office. One Friday afternoon, after English lit and during a free period, he invited Nneoma to his office.

"Ehenn! Remind me what you said your name is. Nn-Nnenna?" guessed Mr. Uka as Nneoma entered. Pretending not to know, he tapped his forehead gently and closed his eyes as if to make the correct guess.

"Nneoma, sir," she corrected. "Have you forgotten so soon? Remember, you asked me not too long ago."

"Yes … yes. It's just that there are too many students in this school to remember all their names. As a teacher, I ought to know and familiarize myself with the serious students who want to succeed. Most of what we have in the classes are nonentities. They only talk and make noise. Call them gasbags, windbags, or chatterboxes … and you are not wrong!" Mr. Uka was trying to impress Nneoma with his vocabulary. He pouted and then gestured with his hands close to his mouth, "Talk, talk … that's all they know."

"Sit down." He pointed to a chair in front of him, across the table from where he sat. "So tell me, Nneoma, where are you from?"

"Umuagu, sir."

"Good! That village seems to produce good girls—obedient and real good girls."

"If you say so, sir."

"Now, I want you to halt this 'sir' thing whenever I am talking to you in a private discussion. I like you, and we can be very useful to each other. If you cooperate, you'll never regret your stay in this school. You are a sweet girl, you know?"

Nneoma was beginning to understand where Mr. Uka was heading, as he also made romantic gestures while he talked. She kept quiet. Mr. Uka took her quietness for acceptance.

"What about coming to my house this weekend—on Sunday?"

"To do what, sir?" Nneoma asked.

At that moment, Mr. Uka stood up and moved to the other side of the table. He sat on the table and leaned closer to Nneoma.

"To know each other much better. To play and have fun by touching ourselves freely and enjoying ..." As Mr. Uka was saying that, he extended his right hand and touched Nneoma on her left breast. Not anticipating anything like that, he withdrew his hand instantly after receiving a sharp slap on his left cheek. He cursed under his breath as Nneoma stood up abruptly and left his office immediately, banging the door hard behind her.

She went back to her classroom. Sitting on her stool and leaning her face onto her folded arms on top of her locker, she began to cry. It was just her second week in the school.

Chapter 9

"I'm Hope," she introduced herself. "I have this letter for both of you." She handed a letter to Nneoma, preferring just to give it to her rather than Onyekachi. She was tall and lanky. She had a long face with a fitting pointed nose. Her mouth was suitable for her long face too, but her eyes were just a little larger in proportion, but not entirely out of proportion. Her eyes were dark brown, and she had long eyelashes. It would be okay to describe her as pretty rather than beautiful. Nneoma took the letter, somewhat stupefied. As if trying to relax their minds, Hope smiled in a friendly manner, revealing a small gap in between the upper set of her fine teeth. "It's from Njideka."

"Are you her friend?" Nneoma asked, not very relaxed.

"Yes. We are neighbors too! Our house is just a stone's throw from theirs. Perhaps you will be surprised, too, if I say that I know both of you well. You are Nneoma, and you're Onyekachi, and both of you are close friends of Njideka's," she said, pointing to Nneoma and then to Onyekachi. "Apart from having seen both of you on one or two occasions when you visited Njideka, she tells me so much about you. She confides so much in me, and that is why she asked me to deliver this letter to both of you. She would have—"

"But Njide left with her father to start her SS in Onitsha after the JSCE long vacation," Onyekachi cut in, a little doubtful.

"Yes. She is now with Madonna Girls' Secondary School in Onitsha. But before she left, she devised a means of communicating with you both. She knew, based on what you discussed together before she left, that both of you would continue with CHSN, and coincidentally, it happens to be my school since JSI. Therefore, she arranged to send letters to both of you through me." Hope was not in a hurry. She was saying the words with ease while repeating and stressing "both of you" as she talked.

"So ... does it mean she posted the letter to us through you?" Onyekachi inquired, not sure. The envelope was blank, making it a little confusing.

"No. Her father visits home every two weeks during the weekend. She sent it through him. To avoid suspicion, she decided to address the letter to me. The letter I gave to Nneoma, though not addressed to any of you, was enclosed together with another separate letter for me, inside another envelope addressed to me. Njideka then directed me in my own letter that the unaddressed letter belongs to you both. The letter was brought to my house on Saturday morning by one of the twin brothers."

Njideka's intention for enclosing the letters in one envelope addressed to Hope was well understood by Onyekachi and Nneoma. But Hope was not done yet.

"This measure has to be taken because even if the letter were addressed to Nneoma to be delivered through me, it might raise suspicion. Lucy and Celia may tamper with it, suspecting something fishy, if you permit me to use the word. They might even expose the contents of the letter that belonged to Onyekachi to their parents. You would agree with me that none of you would like that to happen."

"Are you in SSI too?" Nneoma asked.

"Yes," Hope answered in her usual yes-or-no fashion, pausing before explaining further. "SSIB. My class is next to his." Hope gestured at Onyekachi with her hand, not really looking at him directly.

"So if we reply to this letter," Onyekachi said, pointing to the letter in Nneoma's hand, "how would it get back to her?" He wanted to know the contents of the letter without further delay.

"Yes. That's simple too," Hope replied enthusiastically. "You just leave the envelope unaddressed after sealing. I'll use my own handwriting to address it to her. But one thing you must know is this: if you reply to any letter from her, it will take two weeks at most to reach her. Reason is that her father comes home once every two weeks, as I said earlier. He comes on a Friday evening and leaves early the following Monday morning to go to work. He came home last Friday and left early this morning."

"Invariably, what this means is that whenever Njide replies to any of our letters immediately, it will take another two weeks before it will reach us," Onyekachi remarked dryly.

"Yes, at least for now. Your reply can actually get to her faster if you devise a means to receive the letter from her on the weekend and send back reply same weekend," Hope said consolingly. "There is no better choice for now since the postal system is not effective." The "your" she used was singular. Hope was being helpful and did not pretend about that. From all that she said, it was clear that she knew that the trio of Onyekachi, Nneoma, and Njideka were close friends. She also knew that Onyekachi and Njideka were in love with each other. Onyekachi felt a little embarrassed that she knew so much about them. But she did not seem to be a bad girl; at least he hoped she wasn't.

The long break was not over yet. Nneoma was still holding the letter as they walked along. They intended to open the letter while seated. That would represent a cultured manner rather than opening and reading it while standing or walking on the road. Suddenly, another student intercepted them. Nneoma recognized him instantly. It was Stanley. What on earth did he want from her again? Didn't she tell him she was not interested? Why was he still following her about and embarrassing her?

"What can we do for you?" Onyekachi asked with a hard face.

"*Momen*, what is your business with this girl?" Stanley asked in return. He postured in front of them to stop their forward movement. "Don't you think that you people are deceiving yourselves in believing that you are deceiving others?" He fumed with frustration.

Onyekachi was surprised and angered. He'd never expected that. Initially, he was thinking that he was one of the newly promoted students in SS3, trying to demonstrate his seniority.

"So, lover boy, don't you think it is the best thing to do ... deceive ourselves?" Nneoma sneered.

"You ..." Stanley pointed at Nneoma. "You are even worse. You said that you want to be a reverend sister, yet you're doing abominable things. Who do you think you are deceiving? Why not remove this 'brother-and-sister' thing and lessen your sins by not adding lies?"

"Fantastic, Preacher. So our sins—your sin and my sin—won't be more if I concede to your advances and perhaps give it another name entirely?" Nneoma was exasperated.

Onyekachi came to understand that the boy was one of those boys going after Nneoma. Nneoma had told him earlier. The boy looked like one of the senior students in SS2 or SS3, but the issue at hand did not call for seniority indeed. Onyekachi was prepared to slug it out with him if it came to that. The boy had insulted them.

"Look here," Onyekachi snarled. "I think you are a shameless fool. You chased somebody, and she did not agree. Must you vent your frustration this way? You should be ashamed of yourself, *yeye* boy."

"You dare insult me?" Stanley raged. "I am your senior, and I can assure you that you will find it very uncomfortable in this school. If you don't know me, ask about me. I am Stanley—Stanley De Razor."

"Oh! We are sorry, Senior Stanley De Erased," Nneoma taunted. "Did my brother …? Oh, sorry, my boyfriend … Oh, sorry, my husband … Yes, my husband … Did he insult you? We are sooo sorry, De Erased."

Nneoma had a way of making one look stupid if one deserved it. Onyekachi feared that eventually she would land herself into serious trouble, but she had always gone unscathed. Onyekachi and Nneoma looked at each other like real lovers and laughed loudly, which made Stanley look even more stupid. Stanley clenched his fist as if he wanted to throw a punch. Immediately, Onyekachi pushed Nneoma aside to avert the punch. He took a step backward and balanced himself like a professional boxer waiting for his opponent to throw the first punch before he would release his own deadly blow.

"Come on … come on," Onyekachi urged him with nods. "Maybe it will allow you to let off some steam."

Clearly sensing that he may not be a good match for him in a physical combat, Stanley retreated and muttered, "We shall see." As he was leaving, Nneoma called out to him.

"Hey, De Rave! When will we see you again? We are beginning to enjoy your rants and raves so much!"

Stanley did not look back but continued moving away from them. Onyekachi and Nneoma continued in their direction. On reaching the veranda of the class block, Nneoma opened the envelope, and inside were two separate letters. One was addressed to Onyekachi and the other to Nneoma. Light sheets of a writing pad were used for the letters, which were sealed separately with adhesive tape, done with such artistry that the envelope didn't appear bulky.

"Njide will always be Njide," Nneoma said, studying the letters carefully. You know, I thought it was just one letter inside this envelope. I never thought there could be two letters inside here! And who would have thought otherwise anyway? Poor girl, she has her perfect way of doing things, and she really needs to do it perfectly now that it matters most."

"She's *melsan*, I suppose," Onyekachi added, accepting his own letter from Nneoma.

"Melsan? What does that mean?" Nneoma asked.

"I think you need to read a book on temperament, and then you'd appreciate why people act the way they do," Onyekachi replied. "A senior friend gave it to me." He was carefully peeling off the adhesive tape used to seal his letter.

Nneoma became interested. "That would be nice! So how would you describe me?"

"Wait until you read the book I'll give you. You'll get firsthand information and will be able to tell what temperament you have." Onyekachi did not want to dwell on the topic. If there was anything he was interested in just then, it was reading his letter without further delay.

"Okay, I'm off to my classroom. I still have some time before break is over to see what she has to say," Nneoma said finally, and she left.

The classroom was empty except for a group of three girls sitting around a locker, chatting in low tones. Onyekachi moved to the end of the classroom, farthest from the girls. He sat on a stool and leaned against a wall, relaxing one foot on a nearby locker.

The contents of the letter were words of reassurance and love from Njideka. She was more expressive in the letter than she would have been if she spoke with him face-to-face. She pledged to be true in their relationship and assured him that out of sight was not out of mind; rather, absence would make her heart grow fonder. The contents of the letter were like pills of relief to Onyekachi. He was already feeling her absence greatly in the few weeks at CHSN. He had been thinking about life in the city. He knew what city life was all about. Most people in the city seemed to be living under no moral standards. "This is capable of polluting the most innocent of minds," he thought aloud, fearing for Njideka.

The village wasn't a better place either. Moral decadence seemed to be the order of the day. Onyekachi wasn't surprised when he learned of what transpired when Nneoma responded to Mr. Uka's call to his office. Nothing would be surprising coming from a teacher who made obscene gestures to his own students in the classroom. Onyekachi had persuaded Nneoma not to report him to the principal, giving reasons that included their being new in the school and victimization. A similar thing had happened in their JS. Out of desire for Nneoma, a particular male teacher scored her much more than she was actually supposed to score on an examination, when it was obvious to everyone that nobody would score that high. Moral decadence! It was alarming that older people, expected to be in vanguard against such acts, were also found culpable. Why?

Onyekachi's broodings were cut short by the sound from the giant bell, signifying that the long break was over. He moved over to his rightful seat. Shortly, the classroom would be filled with students and the teacher. In first term SSI, every student was expected to take all subjects. Based on the subjects they performed better, they would select their subjects in second term SSI. Subject combination areas included arts, social sciences, and pure sciences. Onyekachi had already opted for pure sciences and was only doing what was required of him in the first term to prepare ahead for the second term. He must achieve his ambition; he must become a civil engineer, and science subjects represented the foundation.

He knew that one other dream must be realized in his life. He might be too young to think in that respect, but his young mind never ceased to dwell on that: the dream to be united with Njideka forever.

Chapter 10

Mrs. Ikem occasionally visited Eze at Kaduna for her medical checkup. After the death of her husband, she disliked living in Kaduna. It did not even matter that Kaduna was where the family accumulated the wealth that made them a family to reckon with in the community. The late Mr. Ezekiel Ikem was killed in a religious riot on a business trip to another neighboring northern town. His remains were never found. Subsequently, Mrs. Ikem swore never to live in the North again. To buttress her conviction of how insecure it was, religious riots and killings became incessant, and people from the east were mostly the usual targets. They were killed by the hundreds and thousands. She had prayed that Eze would relocate from Kaduna to any of the major eastern cities, like Aba or Onitsha. It would also mean being closer to home. She had tearfully implored her son on several occasions to relocate, but Eze remained adamant and unwilling as he tried to convince his mother to see reason.

"Mama, it's not easy. It may be easy to say 'relocate' to a government worker or any other person, but for a businessman like me, it's not easy at all! This means starting everything afresh—shops, accommodation, business contacts, business style, and so on and so forth! These can cripple a business if not handled well. Mama, please try to understand."

"Ndubueze *nwa m*, are all these excuses more important than your life?" Mrs. Ikem had replied hysterically. "This is an issue of life and death, and you must take it very seriously. During the last riot, the goods in your new shop at the other side of the city were looted, and the shop was burned down completely. Was it not miracle enough that your boy in that shop escaped unharmed? Are you trying to make me understand that a thousand and two hundred slaughtered were not the lives of human beings but those of goats and chickens? Do you want to kill me by your continual stay here?"

Eze had calmed her down by assuring her that he would put additional effort into arranging for relocation to Aba. Although he was tempted to tell her that Kaduna was safer than it was, he knew it would far from placate her. None of Mrs. Ikem's children would do anything to hurt her feelings, Eze inclusive. Lately, she had developed high blood pressure, and upsetting her would only aggravate her condition. However, Eze did not hesitate to tell his mother that the relocation would take some time. He told her that he needed to get some things in place before he would finally relocate.

Mrs. Ikem wished it done immediately. If wishes were horses, beggars would ride! She recalled with a hiss what prompted the family's relocation from home to Kaduna.

The late Ezekiel Ikem had dealt in palm oil. He bought in large quantities, direct from local producers. He stored the palm oil in drums and shipped them to the north. Because he was operating with enough capital, he also bought palm oil in excess, which would be preserved and stored for some months. He had good timing because he knew the seasons in the year when palm oil was cheapest. He took advantage of it, preserving and storing a lot of palm oil when it was cheapest and selling when it was costliest. His business acumen never failed him. He had a knack for business, and everybody liked to deal with him. He also made a lot of profit and was famous.

However, his competitors were not happy. Those who were in the business before him became too embittered by their dwindling fortunes and by the mere fact that he dwarfed them. They conspired among themselves to run his business down. Some resorted to witchcraft, while others connived with Mr. Ikem's boys assigned to ship and supply drums of palm oil in the north to generate false market reports and steal money. The boys began to break loose and form their own businesses. Things were getting bad for Mr. Ikem, and he suffered heavy losses. Finally, he decided to take action. He sacked the remaining boys, who, unknown to him, were also waiting for their time to strike. He started going to the north himself to sell his goods, and much to his chagrin, he discovered that all the reports from his boys were false. Then, from his constant trips north, he discovered new business connections. He rented an apartment in Kaduna when his presence was needed more to manage his growing business. He did much better than before. Gradually, he moved his family with him to Kaduna. He was at the peak of his business career when he met his premature death. For a man of such prominence in his community to be killed and his corpse not found was something worth grieving for. Mrs. Ikem felt like crying, not sure whether for her late husband or for Eze, who was reluctant to relocate.

A year and a half had passed, and there was no sign of relocation yet. It was time for her yearly medical checkup, which Eze took seriously. This was normally done at the teaching hospital. She disliked distant journeys. To her, traveling to Kaduna was a bitter pill, but with the issues at hand, she must swallow it.

It had been five days since Mrs. Ikem left for Kaduna. Two days after she left, teachers went on strike. Onyekachi did not feel his mother's absence much, as Nneoma was there to handle kitchen chores. After first attending to herself in the morning, Nneoma would come over to help Onyekachi, after which they studied together. It was second term SS2. They were already reading ahead of time to be adequately prepared for Senior Secondary Certificate Examination next year. Both had been doing well in their respective subject combination areas—Nneoma in arts; Onyekachi in pure sciences. The only subject Nneoma had been having a problem with was English literature, which Mr. Uka taught. Even though the subject was originally one of her favorites, Mr. Uka was bent on frustrating her. Her interest was waning. If not for her undauntedness, she would have given up on it.

It was mid-morning, and it did not seem as if it was going to be a sunny day. The sky was dull. The weather was cool, and a light wind blew over the place. Everything was quiet except for the flapping of leaves on the trees as the wind moved them. With that kind of weather, it was difficult to say whether it was going to rain. But from all indications, it was not likely to rain because the local Ekeukwu market would be in session. The rainmakers would be expected to be on guard to not allow rain to fall so as not to disrupt market activities. As an *Eke* market day, another local weekday, most people had gone to the Ekeukwu market. Some had left at the wee hours of the morning to do early morning transactions, depending on the kind of goods they wanted or offered for sale. Ekeukwu market was the community's biggest, most significant, and most popular market. It was held once in every eight market days. Whenever Ekeukwu market coincided with a Sunday, the market would be held on *Nkwo* market day, which would be the Saturday before the Sunday. There were four local market days in the local calendar: *Eke, Orie, Afor,* and *Nkwo*. Ekeukwu attracted big market activities, as people from big cities like Umuahia and Aba came to buy and sell.

On Ekeukwu market day, children seldom moved about to play. They played indoors or were restricted within their own compounds. They never fetched water from the stream or firewood in the bush. The day was considered an easy day for child abductors since almost all adults would be at the market, either buying or selling. There were stories in the past about children being abducted on such days and used for rituals.

Nneoma had finished doing the day's chores for Onyekachi. She felt like taking her bath and getting refreshed before going into the reading session with Onyekachi. Being an Ekeukwu market day, the environment was conducive for reading because it was quieter since so many people were away. Nneoma took the things she needed, including a bucket of water, and went to the bathroom to take her bath.

Before she finished taking her bath, Onyekachi prepared himself a cup of tea and enjoyed it with a small loaf of bread. He cleared and cleaned the table and then stretched out on the bed as he waited for Nneoma. Nneoma hardly ate in the morning hours, and if she eventually did, it was very little.

Onyekachi's feelings toward Nneoma were unusual that morning. He had never had such an overpowering attraction to her. The more he tried to focus his mind and attention elsewhere, the more difficult it seemed. As he relaxed on the bed waiting for her, he was battling within himself.

"Kachi, you know Mama's not around and her room is locked." Nneoma paused and continued. "I cannot use her mirror, comb, and cream, so I hope you won't mind if I use yours. I'll not ask for powder because I know boys don't have any." She stood by the door as if waiting Onyekachi's permission before entering the room fully. The towel she'd borrowed from Onyekachi, which she'd tied around her chest, barely covered her thighs adequately. On seeing her thighs, Onyekachi's heart started beating faster.

"It's all yours. Suit yourself," Onyekachi managed to reply, the words sinking in his mouth.

Nneoma moved to the dressing table, which was opposite Onyekachi's bed. Her back was turned to Onyekachi, who was still relaxing on the bed. She faced the standing mirror while combing her hair. Onyekachi gazed at her backside, lustfully surveying her feminine contours. The magnitude of the attraction grew even more, and he developed a compelling urge to grab her.

"You are stunning," he flattered, pretending not to be serious.

"Thank you," Nneoma responded, not suspecting anything. She applied a little amount of Vaseline to her skin and put on her clothes.

"Come on. Get up, Kachi. Remember that you are to teach me in a more comprehensive way how to solve problems in longitude and latitude. Our math teacher did not teach the topic well. We have a lot to cover today so please get up!"

"Don't you think you need a little rest before we start? After all those chores, you need to lie down a little, say, five to ten minutes. Just stretch out on the bed."

"But you know …"

"Yes, I know," he interrupted. "But you need the rest equally. You are not a machine. Machines also need rest, or is that not so?" He pretended to be considerate.

"Okay," Nneoma accepted. She giggled and lay beside Onyekachi, by the outer edge of the bed. Some seconds later, Onyekachi gradually rested his right hand on Nneoma's arm. Moments later, he started stroking her. Nneoma perceived the interpretation and wanted to get up quickly from the bed, but Onyekachi, anticipating such a reaction, held her back.

"Kachi, what is the meaning of this? What are you planning to do?" She was now fully aware of Onyekachi's intention, for he was now pressing his body against hers as if he'd never let go. The strength in him was extraordinary, too much for Nneoma to overcome.

"Kachi, you're hurting me. Don't attempt anything you'll live to regret ..."

A knock followed by a voice calling out in greeting at the door leading to the corridor interrupted Nneoma's plea. The voice was unmistakably Njideka's.

Chapter 11

"Good morning. Is anybody here?" Njideka called in anticipation of a response after knocking yet another three times on the door. "Kachi, are you there?" She stood by the door and waited. If only she knew that Mrs. Ikem was not at home, she would have tiptoed into Onyekachi's room to make her arrival more surprising. She had a lot of respect for Mrs. Ikem and would not want her to think differently of her manners or intended action. The gate and the corridor door where she stood were not locked, which indicated that somebody was inside the house. She wondered why there had not been any response. She knocked again and waited. Finally, when it dawned on her that it was an Ekeukwu market day and Mrs. Ikem may have gone to the market, she decided to proceed to Onyekachi's room. She had hardly entered the corridor when Onyekachi appeared from the other end of the corridor.

"Who's that?" he asked in response. His voice held an air of authority as he pretended not to be aware that it was Njideka.

"Kidnappers!" Njideka joked. "Have you been sleeping inside or what?"

"Oh, Njide, it's you!"

"Maybe my spirit," she joked again, revealing her frustration. "Could that explain why I was not heard since I have been knocking and calling out?"

He caught up with her at the middle of the corridor and welcomed her.

"Sorry, we were just busy trying to solve some problems in math," he lied.

"You mean Nneoma is there too? What of your mother? Has she gone to Ekeukwu market?" As she asked, they walked toward Onyekachi's room.

Njideka had developed significantly into a full-grown woman. She looked gorgeous and graceful, and Onyekachi couldn't help but admire her more. Onyekachi felt fortunate.

"Nneoma, so you are here too?" Njideka said as they entered the room. She observed that her face was not like the usual welcoming bright, smiling face. "What kind of math problem is biting you so hard that you look so gloomy? Couldn't Kachi solve it?"

"No. It's not as if the problem is too difficult. It's just that Nneoma failed to make a good sketch of the globe with the angles of latitude and longitude, hence she was angry with herself," he lied again, not allowing Nneoma to speak for herself.

"Yes," Njideka added in the affirmative, "our math teacher told us that the first step in solving problems correctly in great and small circles is a good sketch. But I don't understand . . . Have you lost your artistic touch, Nneoma?" Njideka was surprised that Nneoma, who used to be one of the best sketch makers in their JS, was finding it difficult to make a good sketch of an ordinary globe.

"So it's also called 'great and small circles'?" Nneoma joined the talk.

"Yes, and it's also called lines of latitude and longitude," Onyekachi began to explain. "Lines of latitude represent small circles; lines of longitude represent great circles." As Onyekachi was still explaining, Njideka dropped her handbag on the reading table and sat on the bed. Moments later, she pulled off her shoes and lay straight, propping herself on two pillows. The action attracted Onyekachi's attention. He knew she couldn't have done that when they were in JS. As he was still looking in her direction, capturing what she was doing, she looked back and smiled to him. He smiled back, recalling that life was a stage.

"I argued it out with my father," she said, changing the topic. "There are indications that the strike action may last for one month or more since the government says that all the teachers' demands cannot be met immediately. And the teachers are not willing to shift grounds either, insisting that their demands must be met before they can call off the strike. They are demanding their three months' unpaid salary arrears, and for better service conditions."

"You really have the main gist about the strike," he said.

"Yes, because I have to convince him. As if it weren't enough, I told him that my mother would need me at home to help out with certain chores."

"It was two days after Mama left for Kaduna that the strike began," Nneoma informed her, not showing interest in what she said.

"It's only six weeks after Njideka left home for Onitsha since the last holiday ended that it began. There will be more time to study on our own this strike period. With ample time, Nneoma will definitely know how to make better sketches." As he said the last words, the impact of the fabrications made Nneoma shoot a glance at him. He cleverly dodged it in time, as if expecting it. After all, he created the fabrications to cover up for the true story.

"Njide, could you please be with him while I go to the house now? I shall be with you both in the next hour or two." She stood up to leave as she made the request.

"Wait, Nneoma. Who are you referring to as 'him'? Your 'brother'?" Njideka queried. She knew Nneoma would not have referred to Onyekachi as "him" instead of "my brother" unless something was wrong, something he was responsible for.

"Nothing, Njide," she responded. "I'll see you later."

Onyekachi's fabrications made her sick, and she knew that her continued stay would betray the situation.

As Nneoma left the room, Mrs. Ikem's advice on her relationship with Onyekachi echoed in her head: "In any relationship, a greater role is expected of the girl. Men are weaker or easily excited, hence they cannot be trusted. Again, considering the fact that you are not blood relatives, temptations may occur." Nneoma could not believe what had happened. She had not taken the words seriously because she'd never thought something like that could happen. Was it that she did not play her role very well? Perhaps she contributed to that, but in any case, Onyekachi must apologize and promise that it would never happen again. She had learned her lesson anyway.

It became obvious to Njideka, judging from the way Nneoma left, that whatever was disturbing her could not have been a mere sketch problem in math. Onyekachi was the culprit.

"What did you do to her?" she asked firmly.

"I don't understand. What do you mean?"

"I asked what you did to Nneoma," she insisted.

"I told you that a problem in math ..."

"Please spare me that. You don't want me to leave immediately too, do you? You must tell me the truth!" Njideka repositioned herself so she was sitting on the bed, silently threatening to go. She paused from putting on her shoes, waiting to hear what Onyekachi said.

"Okay. What happened was that Demo the Casanova summoned her to his office."

"And who is Demo?" she inquired.

"Demonstration. He's our English lit teacher; his real name is Tom Uka."

"Ehenn?" Njideka pressed further.

"Everybody knows he is a womanizer, but he wouldn't shift his eyes away from Nneoma, and he invited her to his office."

"To do what?"

"Hmm. That man? Rapist!"

"Whaaat?" Njideka screamed. "Raped her? Are you saying he raped Nneoma?"

"No, it's not that ... basically," he corrected. "It's just that he attempted to fondle her, but she gave him a dirty slap. But the main problem she had with me was that after she told me what happened, I scolded and teased her seriously for even daring to enter Demo's office in the first place. But she said that she didn't know Demo was that bad. She then chided me for insinuating that she was a loose girl. Although I realized my error and pleaded for her forgiveness, she was already too angry."

"But, Kachi, you would not expect Nneoma to do otherwise, would you?" Njideka was calming down.

"No! That's why I pleaded with her."

Onyekachi could not have believed that he could be so masterful in telling convincing lies. But lies they were ... and no credit for him at all! Once a lie was told, other lies were needed to cover up the first ... and so on. One would always be in constant fear that the truth would be known eventually, some time or some day.

"Okay, we'll see her together before I leave today. Everything will be all right," Njideka assured. Onyekachi was momentarily relieved but also knew that it wasn't yet over. He prayed inwardly that Nneoma would not be around when Njideka was leaving. He was certain that Nneoma would not come back to meet them. Whatever happened, he was confident, however, that she would not tell Njideka the real story.

Onyekachi was already regretting the act. He knew that such an act, if not stopped, could result in pregnancy, which was forbidden, as village tradition would not allow intermarriage. Young people had reasoned that such tradition should be abolished. They argued that people that are ripe for marriage, girls mostly, suffered more. In some instances, although they could easily find suitors in their own villages where they grew up and socialized, the girls were at the mercy of unsuitable men from other villages. Sometimes they got their suitors through recommendations from older people. Such marriages did not usually work out as expected.

Young people had argued consistently that recommendations and the matchmaking methods in marriage were old school. They opined that marriage should be built on love and understanding, which must develop over time in a relationship. Marriage should not be through recommendation or imposition just to fulfill an obligation. On the other hand, the village elders argued that tradition must be passed on to them and upheld. They feared that their ancestors would punish them severely if they did otherwise and allowed village intermarriages. They blamed the youths for being crazy with modernization and little or no regard for tradition. They believed that tradition and modernization moved in opposite directions, which was the reason that things that worked for them seemed not to work for the new generation.

It was in the spirit of enforcing tradition that a boy and the girl he impregnated were forced to perform a ritual offering. The offering was meant to cleanse the land so that the girl could deliver her baby. Initially, the couple objected to make the offering on the grounds that they were Christians, instead requesting that they be joined in marriage. Their request angered the elders more, who also claimed to be Christians. After threatening to deal with them and their families, which included exclusion, the couple succumbed. To some people, that was funny because there had been pregnancies of such that were actually aborted secretly that the elders did not know. The land was not cleansed for those pregnancies, and yet nothing disastrous happened.

Onyekachi regretted his action. His major regret was that he had betrayed the trust Nneoma had for him. It was a shame that he tried such a thing on the girl who regarded him, without any reservation, as a brother. He had behaved like someone who had no guiding principles or self-control. He wished it had never happened.

"What's life going to be like after secondary school?" he asked, desperate to change the topic after a long silence separated them.

"To get a university education, of course. What do you think?"

"Yes! And after that become an engineer, get a good job, and as God would have it, be united ..." He intentionally paused, waiting to hear what she would say or add.

"We're back to it. What if after becoming accomplished, you decide to dump me for some obscure reason?" Njideka asked, touching him. It was with all elements of seriousness, though she was smiling to make it look casual. Onyekachi flinched.

"You can't be serious, Njide. You know I love you and can't do that. I have a conscience—active and alive."

"You know I'm no longer a girl of those JS days. We've come a long way, Kachi. I don't even want to imagine that, but sometimes it's good to."

"So why do you ask?"

"To face reality. Though it has not happened, I pray it will not. But I don't think it is a bad idea to think that it could happen. I don't know how I would survive if it happens." She looked into his eyes. "You are my Prince Charming, my first and only love. I will do my own part; I will never disappoint or break your heart, as I have remained a faithful friend."

"You know me more than that too. You are my angel. I love and respect you. That is why it is in my subconscious not to fool around." He felt guilty remembering what had happened earlier. However, he was happy that he was stopped before things got out of hand. He could still lift his head high for not fooling around. He was happy that they were reserving themselves for each other.

Like people struck by Cupid's arrow, they talked mainly about their love for each other. They also talked about their aspirations, the future, and their academics. After about three hours, Njideka finally decided it was time for her to leave. Both of them walked down to Nneoma's to see her, but she was not available. Onyekachi muttered inwardly, *Thank God.*

"Kachi, please tell Nneoma that I'll see her sometime next week if the strike continues. I can't wait for her because it's getting late."

"I'll do that. But even if the strike is called off before next week, I'll still be receiving messages of hope because Hope is there," Onyekachi punned.

"Yes, surely and continuously. But ... point of correction: messages of total assurance," she said.

Chapter 12

Finally, Eze relocated to Aba. Things were getting difficult. When it was time to register Onyekachi and Nneoma for SSCE, Mrs. Ikem handled it without asking Eze for money. She got the money from a savings account that she'd had since her heyday in business. She played an active role in the wholesale, distribution, and retail of expensive fabrics like lace, *george*, and *hollandaise*, which womenfolk used for making beautiful blouses, wrappers, and so forth.

Mrs. Ikem was fascinated by the way Onyekachi and Nneoma were studying for SSCE. They formed a perfect reading pair and read with determination and vigor.

When Eze took SSCE, the family was together. He was not much of a bookworm. His mind was preoccupied with starting a business. He did not intend to further his education. He just wanted to finish secondary education so he wouldn't be dubbed a dropout. Though Eze wanted a good result, he did not sacrifice much. Olachi took SSCE in Lagos while living with Auntie Kate. Though her result was good, Mrs. Ikem was not there to see how she prepared. Even with her good result, it was two years before she was admitted to the university. Olachi was a part three student of sociology. Grace sat for SSCE in Port Harcourt. She was science-inclined, and her result was good.

Mrs. Ikem learned from Uncle Sam that she was very studious. She was aware that from childhood, Grace had loved reading, but she had never seen her read in preparation for an external examination like SSCE. It was coincidental that both Grace and Uncle Sam shared a reading habit. Uncle Sam had bookshelves in his living room, adorned with a variety of books arranged according to their different topics. Grace started living with Uncle Sam immediately after their father's death. She was in her second year of medical school at the university. Carol was in SSI at Aba with Eze. Although she always came first in the class, she had never demonstrated an impressive reading habit.

For the umpteenth time, Mrs. Ikem regretted that the family was not together. The family sometimes gathered during festive seasons like Christmas, sometimes staying together for days before dispersing. Mrs. Ikem did not like the arrangement, but she could not do anything about it.

Mrs. Ikem had always urged Onyekachi and Nneoma not to read too late in order to enable them to wake up in time for school the following day. More often, Nneoma found it convenient to sleep at Onyekachi's, as it afforded them more time to read together.

The reconciliation came fast after the incident. She'd come to him two hours after Njideka left.

"Kachi, I have come to apologize for what happened. I'm sorry," she had said.

Onyekachi was dumbfounded at first. "But . . . I-I should be the one to do the apologizing."

"I think I should do it first. The blame doesn't go to you alone. I have a share of the blame too. We are both to blame." She paused and then continued. "But you must promise me . . ."

Onyekachi knelt before her remorsefully. "I'll promise you anything."

"Promise me that it'll never happen again. As for me, I have decided not to think about that again … and you have to give me your word."

He did promise her, as expected, and pleaded for her forgiveness too. She became cheerful again and tried to put everything that happened behind them. However, she started watching her actions closely to preempt any nondeliberate act that may excite him sexually. Onyekachi proved to be trustworthy once again.

SSCE was starting in three weeks. Preparation was in full swing for Onyekachi and Nneoma. On a Thursday night, which was typically quiet, they were coincidentally reading the same topic. The study was interactive. They exchanged ideas as they discussed the topic. The following day was going to be Eid-el-Maulud holiday for the nation, so there would be no need to hurry to bed earlier because there would be no school. Mrs. Ikem had already gone to bed.

"My back is aching. I've been bending for too long. Permit me to relax on the bed for a minute." Nneoma moved to the bed and lay down near the outer edge, propping on two pillows. She faced upward, inclining her head so that she could make use of the light to read the book she held over her face. Onyekachi was still engrossed with what he was reading. He rarely considered recreation or some sort of break until he was done, which Nneoma often criticized. He was determined to conclude the topic and move on to another one, probably a mathematics topic. He loved solving mathematical problems and used them as a tonic whenever he was getting bored and tired of reading.

Shortly, the book Nneoma was holding hit the floor. She had fallen asleep. He picked it up and put it on the reading table among the other books. He continued to concentrate on what he was doing.

The room was getting quieter, and the only noise was his flipping the pages of his book. He no longer heard the occasional noise from neighboring households preparing late dinners. The quietness was sleep inducing.

He looked at Nneoma, who was sleeping peacefully like a baby, and thought that she deserved it. After doing double chores—for herself and his mother—she must have been exhausted. He decided to allow her to sleep for a while before he woke her to join him in reading.

Seconds ticked into minutes, and his eyes were getting heavy. He thought that what he needed was a break for a few minutes. There were more things to cover. Just a few minutes to relax his head, then he would bounce back to action. Though quite unlike him, he would usually end for the night and go to bed. Quietly, he crept into the bed, which was wide enough to accommodate two people. He never wanted to wake Nneoma or worse still, embarrass her while creeping into the bed. He positioned himself on the inner side of the bed, maintaining enough space between himself and Nneoma.

"Safe distance," he muttered to himself. He was not bothered since he believed that he would get up from the bed in just a couple of minutes, before she awoke. After all, he was not going to sleep. Hardly had he finished calculating the amount of minutes the break would last before he was asleep.

In her usual way, Mrs. Ikem awoke in the middle of the night. It was after midnight. She outstretched her hand and pressed an electric switch on the wall by her bedside, and the room was instantly illuminated. She never liked sleeping with lights on, however dim. The effort of the community in replacing the bad electrical transformer had yielded fruits. Electricity had been restored again after one year of no electricity. For that, Mrs. Ikem would not have to search for where she kept her matchbox to light up her lantern. She noticed that the light in Onyekachi's room was still on.

"Can these children still be awake and reading this late even if they were at Cambridge which many considered as the citadel of learning?" she asked herself, a little worried that they were overstretching it. She stood up and moved to Onyekachi's room.

As she entered the room, her eyes were directed to the bed in which Onyekachi and Nneoma lay. The gap between them had closed up. She started thinking, wondering if what she was seeing was by design or accident. She knew better than to quickly jump to conclusions. She had known the boy and the girl always behaved like brother and sister, but that did not mean that they were, actually. They would be asking for temptation to sleep in the same bed. Nneoma had been using Carol's room whenever she slept over. It quickly became obvious to Mrs. Ikem that it must have happened by accident, however. From the door that was not locked, light still on, and the books scattered on the table, it was evidently clear. She tapped the two of them on the legs, one after the other. Neither woke. Again, she tapped a little harder, this time with both hands—one hand for each person—three consecutive times and simultaneously too.

"Yes . . . yes. Tomorrow is *Sallah* holiday," Onyekachi said sleepily referring to Eid-el-Maulud holiday, and responding to what he thought was the routine of his mother waking him so he could get to school on time.

Nneoma did get up, saying, "Good morning, Mama. I think I should quickly go and sweep the compound." She thought it was already morning.

Mrs. Ikem smiled with amusement.

SSCE had come and gone. Results were being awaited. Onyekachi did not want to take any chances because he knew that the examination council board could be unpredictable at times, hence he registered immediately for the General Certificate of Education (GCE). GCE was an O level examination for external candidates in the form of SSCE. The external candidates didn't have to register with a school, just as required before taking SSCE. Both examinations served the same purposes. Some bright students who'd missed out in the past were frustrated when their results were canceled or seized through no fault of theirs. They had to wait for another year to register. Both examinations were taken once a year, GCE being taken few months after SSCE.

Preparing for and taking the GCE would not be so demanding since what he read for SSCE was still fresh in his memory. The only examination that would require more concentration and time to prepare was the University Matriculation Examination (UME). A different examination board conducted it, and it seemed a little advanced. Onyekachi had already bought the UME form but had not completed it. He was undecided as to the choice of universities to fill in. He was considering universities in the western part of the country.

Nneoma did not need UME to enter a convent. She only required good grades in her O level papers to be eligible. The best she could do as she awaited her result was to pray for good grades, mostly for the required subjects. Mrs. Ikem had been doing her best to support her.

"I've discussed this with Reverend Father Bekee, and he is willing to assist," she announced as she stepped onto the veranda. "He will give the necessary recommendation as the priest in charge of our local parish, but he was emphatic about making good grades." She was telling this to Nneoma, who was playing the game Ludo with Onyekachi on the veranda.

"That won't be a problem, Mama. By the grace of God, Nneoma and I will make the best results in our school." Onyekachi could not hide his excitement for the news. He hoped for the best for her; that that would give her satisfaction and accomplishment in life.

"Thank you, Mama. We did our best in the exams, and all things being equal, I don't see why we shouldn't get more As than Cs. I am very optimistic about that."

"Yes. You sacrificed a lot for the exams. You denied yourselves sleep, rest, and even food. I know you wouldn't be playing Ludo if you still had to take the exam. You know the saying 'All work and no play makes Jack a dull boy'? I think it's your time to play!"

"Yes, Mama," Onyekachi agreed. "We also know that all play and no work makes Jack a mere toy. Remember that I still have UME and GCE to take. I am not entirely free."

"There we are! Who would want to use all his or her time to play? Everything has a limit," she advised. "What about Njideka? It's been quite long since I saw her last."

"She came back from Onitsha last week. She sent word that she will be visiting today," Nneoma replied.

"Good. I'd like to see her when she comes. I shall be off to the mission soon."

Mrs. Ikem entered her room to get herself prepared. Onyekachi and Nneoma started whispering to each other. They were wondering why she asked to see Njideka.

Thirty minutes later, while Onyekachi and Nneoma were on the sixth round of play, Njideka arrived. She alighted from an okada, which stopped in front of the gate. She had lost some weight, probably due to stress relating to exams. However, her face was bright and all smiles.

"Who's winning?" she asked in a loud, excited voice as she entered the gate.

"And who do you think is winning?" Onyekachi replied, bragging.

She met them at the veranda. "Ahhhh! But Nneoma is almost winning this one." She joined them as an observer but in support of Nneoma.

"Don't mind, Njide. I am going to win this one to level up; three for me and three for him," Nneoma assured.

"But don't forget that it's not over until it's over," Onyekachi reminded them. "That's what a game is all about anyway."

Njideka took a seat next to Nneoma.

"Njide, I'm beginning to suspect that my brother is cheating in this game. Each time I level up, he takes the lead again."

"Sure … Kachi?" Njideka quizzed.

"No, it's not so. She has been alert, watching my actions. I didn't cheat, even though some people still argue that cheating is part of the game. Such people believe it's only smart people who can cheat in a game and get away with it!" Onyekachi said with a laugh.

"No! Cheating is stealing, and it's not good," Nneoma cried out.

The game progressed. Everybody was watching with keen interest. Against all expectations that Nneoma would win, Onyekachi eventually won. Nneoma had no other excuse for not winning. She put the Ludo aside, promising revenge some other time.

"So how did the exam go?" Onyekachi asked. He moved from his position and sat beside Njideka on the couch kept on the veranda for relaxation. He took her hand, tucking it into the crook of his arm.

"Stress. Plenty of stress," Njideka replied.

"I can see that already. It shows on your body," Nneoma said.

"Well, I thank God it's over, and by God's grace, I've taken SSCE once and for all."

"And that leaves us with UME. Have you started reading for that?"

"Kachi, you should have asked if I've filled out the form first."

"Hmm. So what are you waiting for?" Nneoma asked. "I learned that the last day for submission is Friday of next week."

"I'm waiting for your brother," Njideka replied demurely.

"Why are you waiting for my brother?"

"I want us to be in the same university. I want to know the choices of universities he made while filling out his form so that I can do the same."

"I've not filled out mine either. I have not decided on choices of universities either!"

"That makes two of us then. So let's take Eastern University as first choice and State University as second choice."

"Okay. Your wish is my command," he acquiesced as he stood up and bowed in a theater-like performance of one bowing before a queen.

"I think I have not seen any two people more compatible than you," Nneoma confessed. "I believe my brother would make the best husband for you, Njide, and I am not flattering you."

Njideka turned her head and gave a sharp look at Nneoma, seeming surprised to hear that. As their eyes met, all of them laughed together.

"Yes ... yes, lest I forget, Mama said you should see her before you leave today."

"You are kidding me, aren't you?"

"Serious. We were with Mama before she left for a mission meeting."

"Yes, she's right. Mama asked to see you. We don't know why."

Njideka was getting excited. It was the first time that Mrs. Ikem had asked to see her personally.

Chapter 13

Things were not getting better for Eze. Managing two big shops stocked with different kinds of electronics at Kaduna, he now struggled to keep one in Aba. However, Mrs. Ikem never regretted the role she played, which was consequential for his relocation. She often told herself that it would be meaningless to amass wealth that one would not live to enjoy. The priceless value she attached to life prompted her to name her first child *Ndubueze*, meaning "life reigns supreme." A woman of firm belief and strong will, she would not be intimidated by her own actions. She was optimistic that things would get better, and that after every storm, the calm would come.

Among the persons badly hit by the condition of things in the family was Nneoma. Some of Nneoma's mates, including Onyekachi and Njideka, were already in different universities and other institutions of higher learning. But while they were studying one course or another, Nneoma was at home, waiting for the dictates of fate. As she'd predicted, she'd cleared all her papers with As and Cs, except in English lit, where she made a P. Reverend Father Bekee was transferred to another distant parish a week before the results were released. Mrs. Ikem's current financial strength was not able to carry both Nneoma and Onyekachi along completely and single-handedly at that level. Things may have been different if Father Bekee were around to make the recommendation and request support from the congregation.

Although Onyekachi had gained admission into the university, he was unable to study civil engineering with his SSCE result. The result for the physics paper was canceled for all the students in the science class where he belonged, and physics was part of the required subjects to study any engineering course. Physics was required with at least a C grade. On the day they took the Physics Theory Paper B, the invigilator caught two candidates cheating with materials they'd concealed and brought into the examination hall. The two candidates were eventually asked to complete and sign the irregularity forms before they were allowed to continue with the examination. The materials were seized. It then came as a shock to hear after the exam that the invigilator was waylaid and beaten after he refused to be bribed and withdraw the forms. Ultimately, it turned out to be an examination center problem; therefore, the physics results were canceled.

Onyekachi cried foul. He reasoned that the punishment for the sins of two persons should not have been meted out to others. But who would listen to him? Nevertheless, he was hopeful that he would make it up with the GCE result, which was about to be released. But the straw that broke the camel's back was the radio announcement that his examination center's physics and chemistry results were withheld due to massive cheating. Although Onyekachi had an acceptable score in the UME, which would have been able to facilitate his admission to study civil engineering, he could not be admitted into the department. It was impossible for him to be admitted to an engineering course without physics. Physics was one of the core prerequisite subjects that required at least a C grade. What luck!

He decided to use what he had. He used his O level subject combination to go for Accountancy in his second choice: State University. He did that for the following reasons: the head of the department was a family friend who would assist him since he did not choose the course while completing the UME form; he did an additional commercial subject in O level, which made him eligible for the course; and he wanted a course that involved calculation as a substitute to civil engineering.

Yet he was not done with his ambition of studying civil engineering. He prayed fervently that the withheld results would be released later. He had also concluded plans to register for another GCE the following year, in the event the withheld results were not released. Results could be withheld indefinitely, and when they were eventually released, they sometimes turned out to be bad. He did not want to remain at home to wait for his plans to work out, hence he decided to spend his time studying Accountancy. It could take another year or two, but he was determined to get there. But Onyekachi also thought it wise to put in his best while studying Accountancy in the interim.

Njideka had no problem whatsoever in persuading her father to allow her to study theater arts. Although he preferred law, he allowed her to make her own choice. Her admission into Eastern University was devoid of any rigorous process since she made it on merit. She also cleared all her papers in SSCE and made the second best result in her school. She had already settled down on campus.

Being her first year in the university, things were happening fast. There were so many activities to indulge in. It appeared that there was never enough time to do the things one wanted or meant to do. Based on that, an orientation program called "Time Management" was organized for freshers by the university. The university environment was such that one was free to opt for what one wanted to do. Nobody stopped anyone from doing anything as long as it did not collide with the rules and regulations of the university.

Things were happening fast in this excitement-inducing environment. The ill wind was also blowing in it too—an environment where people coerced and manipulated or even convinced others to belong to a cult or "group"; an environment where many lost their morality too soon under the guise of being the movers and shakers—the so-called "bigger boys" and "bigger girls" on campus.

"Kachi, I may not visit again this semester," Njideka said.

"Why? What could be the reason for that?" Onyekachi asked in consternation. It was not as if the distance separating their respective campuses was much. It was only a taxi ride, which did not cost much. The two campuses were located in the same city. It was only the second time Njideka visited, while he had visited her about four times.

"I am always very busy ... so many activities, parties, and shows. I rarely have time."

"Njide, do you go partying?"

"And what is wrong with that? Were you not told that while you pass through the university, you should allow the university to pass through you as well?"

"Njide, please don't misunderstand that. It doesn't mean that you must make yourself available for all functions or parties on campus."

"What's wrong with going to parties?"

"I don't mean that going to parties is wrong; it depends on the kind of party. Birthday parties? Departmental parties? Or are they the supposed vibrant events called "hot pants and hot legs," and other activities around campus that were designed to influence one negatively? So tell me, Njide, which one are you talking about?" Onyekachi looked straight into her eyes the way a detective would do when quizzing a criminal to establish the truth.

Njideka turned her face away and kept quiet. Onyekachi moved a bit away from her and faced another direction as if to absorb the shock of the unprecedented change he noticed in Njideka. For the first time, Njideka had argued with him over what seemed absurd. To think that Njideka reasoned the way she did was rather disheartening. To say Onyekachi was shocked was an understatement.

After Njideka left, Onyekachi was moody and worried. It was just the first semester of their first year in the university. He did not want to imagine that she was being influenced negatively so soon. He tried to convince himself that Njideka was just under pressure to adjust to the new environment. *With time, she will understand and be herself again,* one part of him said. He was just beginning to accept that when another part of him asked, *What about you? Are you not also new in the system?*

Onyekachi muttered some prayer to God for the sake of Njideka.

It was the third week since the second semester started. Njideka had not visited, and she did not visit during the vacation as she usually did during their SS. Two days before her examinations last semester, Onyekachi had made time to get her a lovely examination success card. Though he did not spare much time during the visit because of his own exam preparation, delivering the card to Njideka mattered a lot to him.

In the fourth week of resumption, when it became unbearable, he decided to pay her a visit.

He got to the female hostel and had a little problem with a porter. His anxiety to see Njideka had made him forget the visiting hours, which lasted between twelve noon and six in the evening. He was embarrassed when an impolite porter stopped him when, in his haste, he tried to pass the porter's lodge. It took the intervention of another porter to calm the situation. The polite porter advised him to wait for another hour and a half, when it would be visiting hours.

He waited in front of the hostel and refreshed himself with a soft drink and snacks at a nearby kiosk. At the right time, they allowed him in. Upon knocking and entering the room, he saw only Chichi, Njideka's cornermate. The big room was divided with curtains into four parts or corners. The curtains were held by a wooden framework to make it rigid. Each corner had its own bunk bed, wardrobe, table and chairs, and maintained its privacy. Students living in the same corner referred to themselves as cornermates while other members of the room not living in the same corner were referred to as roommates. Chichi was reading at a small table in her corner.

"Hi, Chichi. How've you been?" Onyekachi asked.

"Fine," Chichi replied. She stood up and pulled the other chair up to the table. Njideka used the chair mostly. "Sit down, please. Let me get you a soft drink from the common room."

"No ... thanks. I've just had one."

"Seems you've been around for some time."

"Yes. It didn't occur to me that it's Saturday. I came at the wrong time, so I had to wait. Where's Njide?"

"Oh, she left with Tony by nine in the morning. I guess it was pre-arranged because she actually told me that Tony was waiting for her in front of the hostel."

"Sorry, but who is Tony?"

"He's one of the so-called bigger boys on campus. A fourth-year civil engineering student."

"So what's his relationship with Njide?" Onyekachi asked, trying as much as possible to be calm.

"I'm sorry that you may not like to hear this, but I feel you need to ... because the earlier you know, the better." Chichi paused and then continued, "I'm not sure if Njideka still has the same feelings for you as you do for her."

"So what about this Tony you mentioned?" Onyekachi asked, still trying to be calm.

"Tony is supposed to be in the field doing his six months' IT as an engineering student, but he wouldn't—because to him, money does everything. He is a Casanova who would use gifts and money to turn any girl's head. They say that he isn't from a very well-to-do family, so how he gets the kind of money he throws around baffles me. This is my second year on this campus, and I can say with certainty that Tony is bad news. Nobody likes to interfere in his affairs. He likes it so much with freshers. Njideka seemed to me a good girl when I first met her, but it's as if she's gone completely haywire since she met Tony. She wouldn't listen to me ... Of course, she feels I am jealous of her! Maybe she might listen to you based on the relationship you two shared."

Onyekachi was totally bemused and devastated by all that Chichi said. For a moment, he thought he was dreaming. To confirm he was not, he pinched himself. Had Chichi said "the relationship both of you shared"? Had Njideka told her already that she had quit the relationship? For a moment, Onyekachi felt he wanted to die if it was true. He wished that Chichi were only kidding him. He was still trying to absorb the shock when Njideka arrived.

"Kachi, you did not inform me you were coming today, did you?" she asked formally and dryly.

"I thought I should bring this letter from Nneoma. She was worried that you haven't visited for some time." Onyekachi dropped the letter on the table for her as Chichi left the corner to give them more space and some privacy.

"Please. Nneoma should understand that those days are gone. I am now preoccupied with more pressing things," she almost shouted.

"But, Njide, do I have to give you notice before I visit you?" he asked. He could not bear her first remark any longer.

Njideka frowned and replied, "Yes, of course! This is a civilized world. You may be an embarrassment to some people."

It was becoming too much for Onyekachi, and he was about to explode with anger.

"What has come over you, Njide? Are you under a spell or something, or is it that—?"

"Hey, punk, what are you doing to my baby?" Tony interrupted him with his unannounced arrival. He looked quite mean.

"Hi, Tony." Njideka smiled at him.

"Who's this *chaffman*?" Tony opted for an insulting word used on campus by cultists for someone who lacked courage and strong belief.

"Oh, he was a childhood friend."

"Okay, guy." Tony patted Onyekachi on the shoulder. "Don't get her worked up or I might be tempted to fix you or twist your neck."

Onyekachi felt anger upsurge in himself to hit Tony, but he held back. Not minding the consequences, he was convinced that he could deal with the intruder decisively if they engaged in a physical combat. But then, it was a university. Previously, he had fought on behalf of Njideka, with her solidly behind him. He was almost fighting again because of her, while she was in support of his opponent. What a crazy world!

"Baby," Tony continued, "I need to fill my fuel tank. I hope you enjoyed yourself today. The cruising ride was worth it with an angel like you by my side. See you later."

Njideka nodded with smiles, and having said that, Tony left the corner.

"What is the meaning of this, Njide?" Onyekachi asked.

"Sorry, Kachi. Tony has done so much for me, and I cannot ignore him. I think he's the best thing that has happened in my life lately, and I think it's right to reciprocate the gestures by accepting him too."

"Please, Njide. You can't do this to me. What about the promises? The promises you made to me. The promises we made to each other." As Onyekachi was reminding her of this, he was at the point of shedding tears.

Njideka started laughing. "Childhood fantasies. When I met Tony, I suddenly realized that they were all childhood fantasies. You'll agree with me someday."

"Please ... Njide, this is no fantasy. I love you and will love you forever. Don't allow ..."

"I'm sorry, Kachi. I think you should leave now. Tony will not be happy to see you here again if he comes back. I'm sorry."

All attempts in trying to bring Njideka back to her senses were futile.

Two and a half months had passed; Onyekachi was still an emotional wreck. His love had been scorned and ridiculed. His hopes had been dashed to pieces, and he was unable to concentrate. He had never felt so forsaken and lonely. He tried on many occasions, with lovely cards, to get Njideka to return to her senses, but she had withdrawn completely from him. His heart was broken into irretrievable pieces. For him, love was a bitter experience—a very bitter experience. He started praying to God to give him the grace to forget about Njideka, at least to be spared of the emotional trauma he was going through.

His examinations were just around the corner.

Chapter 14

There were times, or so it seemed, when people were hardly offered even the least of their desires in life. Such was Nneoma's case. After staying two and a half years at home without entering the convent, it began to dawn on her that her greatest ambition was gradually becoming a mirage. She could not even attend any of the least competitive tertiary institutions around. Things did not improve for Mrs. Ikem and family. Uncle Jonah had since ignored her completely. Her maternal people always complained of tough times. Marriage was the only thing Uncle Jonah was interested in about Nneoma, and it seemed it was going his way.

Suitors had been coming for her hand in marriage, but Nneoma rejected them. It was not as if she were too young for marriage; she just wasn't predisposed to it. Then there was Max, the youngest of all the suitors. He never relented.

After completing his National Youth Service, Max got a job immediately with the Town Planning Authority with which he did his primary assignment in the Federal Capital Territory. He was fortunate that they retained him after his primary assignment. Many people scrambled, while some even used political lobbying, to canvass for jobs for their relatives and friends with the Town Planning Authority because of its lucrative work nature. In less than one year, he already had a car of his own and lived in a well-furnished three-bedroom flat in the heart of Abuja. Being his parents' only son, he had been under pressure from his parents and close relatives to get married. He rejected all the girls his parents recommended for him. He knew that marriage was binding forever, and he did not want to marry the wrong person. He wanted to discover "TRe and TLo" in his potential wife. TRe and TLo was Max's coinage for trust, mutual respect, tolerance, and love. These qualities went alongside mutual understanding, which he discovered to be altogether essential for a happy and enduring marriage. Despite the pressure on him, Max was not in a hurry to find a wife.

Max met Nneoma for the first time in the village when he was still a corps member. It was during the yuletide, and most people were at home for celebrations. Initially, Max approached her for friendship, but she rejected him modestly, without hurting his ego. Max was struck by her demeanor and was determined not to give up. It took Max some time to prove to her that all he wanted was a decent relationship with her. Nneoma eventually accepted, but not without caution. Before he left for Abuja after the yuletide, he learned more about Nneoma.

After his National Youth Service, Max started coming home regularly, wooing Nneoma. Before long, Nneoma began to feel what she had not felt for any man before—she started falling in love. When the feeling was getting stronger and stronger, she could no longer hide it and couldn't help but reciprocate Max's overtures. Over a period of time, Max proved to be a true friend to her. Despite all the gossip and insinuations by detractors about Nneoma and her family, he was not scared in any way. He truly showed that he loved her, and that was what mattered. Nearly a year after his National Youth

Service, they were joined as man and wife in both the traditional and church marriage.

Max stayed for one more week in the village after the white wedding and hurried back to Abuja for an official assignment. Nneoma stayed behind at home, planning to join him two days later. She wanted to take care of some things as well as have a discussion with Onyekachi. She would not feel satisfied joining Max without having an intimate talk with Onyekachi first.

Onyekachi was present at the wedding but left immediately after the reception. His semester examinations were imminent, and he had to prepare for them. He was one of the best students in the accountancy department, and he wanted to maintain his position or, better still, improve on it. It meant that he had to devote extra time to academic work, especially with about a year left to finish the program. His studies were the only thing that kept him busy enough to help forget the disappointments of his past. Sometimes he thought that life was a joke—or fantasy, as Njideka had said. Life was full of shattered or unfulfilled dreams. The GCE he registered for was again another huge disappointment, as he could not take Physics Theory Paper B. Physics was the only reason why he'd registered the second time. He didn't know that the examination date for the paper was moved back for political reasons and he missed taking it. He hardly listened to the news on campus, as this would have kept him informed about the change of date. With more financial worries making it difficult to register for yet another GCE, Onyekachi had no option other than to embrace fully the course he was already studying.

"Kachi, I thought you would have stayed at least two more days after my wedding," Nneoma said, expressing her disappointment.

She sat on the lower bunk bed. As a 300 level student Onyekachi was allocated the lower bunk bed rather than an upper bunk bed, usually allocated to lower-level students. There were sixteen occupants in the big room, which was originally designed to accommodate eight students. Eight students were officially assigned to the room while eight other students were being accommodated by the official eight. The eight students that were accommodated were referred to as "squatters" in adopted campus terminology. As usual, there were four corners in the room. Hostel accommodations had been a problem for universities and other higher institutions of learning. There were usually more students than accommodations provided. After exchanging pleasantries, and as a matter of courtesy, two other occupants of Onyekachi's corner left, one after the other, to give Onyekachi and Nneoma some privacy.

"Nneoma, let me welcome you first before you begin to complain, please," he responded. He stood by his reading desk and asked, "What do I offer you?" Then he continued with a smile. "You know, as the local saying goes: 'It's only an unintelligent person who does not know that his sister is a guest.' This means that I have to offer something to you the way I would do to a guest."

"Not to worry ..."

But in a flash, Onyekachi had already left the room. He knew that Nneoma would attempt to stop him from buying her a soft drink, as she would want him to save the money for some other thing because students were in constant need for money, however small. He knew that some refreshment would be good for her after the journey. He came back with a bottle of soft drink and opened it immediately with a bottle opener that he also used as a key ring. He placed the soft drink before her. She looked at it as if she didn't need it but did hold it on her lap in readiness to enjoy it.

"When we met Mama the day after our wedding and she said you'd left, I felt bad," Nneoma said. She pushed toward Onyekachi a big polyethylene bag containing a food flask with assorted fruits and snacks, including two big loaves of bread.

Onyekachi's eyes popped as he scrutinized the contents. "Wow!" he shouted. "There is no more buka for one one one today, including cornermates."

One one one . . . What can that mean? Nneoma wondered.

"Yes!" He then pointed to the contents of the polyethylene bag. "These things mean that there will be no canteen for a full day—morning, afternoon, and evening—for me and my cornermates!"

"But this can't be enough considering that the *jollof* rice in the food flask . . ."

"Who told you that it's not enough? For us students, this is enough—more than enough!" Onyekachi was emphatic.

"Maybe I would agree with you if you say you guys can manage this for lunch and dinner because it seems to me you've had your breakfast already," Nneoma concluded. She switched over to her main concern initially. "So . . . why did you leave immediately . . . just like that?"

"The truth is that I was set to take a test the following day, after which our lecture-free week commenced, which ushered us into exams on Thursday."

"But you could have told me instead of leaving unceremoniously like that."

"Nneoma, you wouldn't want to be distracted, would you?"

"Hey! Has it gotten to the stage where suddenly my brother has become a distraction to me because I'm getting married?"

"No, that's not what I mean. You may not understand. That's why I asked Mama to explain everything to you, and I hope she did. However, I am sorry about that." He held her hand. "I hope my apology pacifies you."

"It was a disappointment when Max and I went to see you and Mama but were greeted by your absence."

"Pleeeease forgive. I said I'm sorry," he implored again. "So where is Max now?"

"He has gone back to Abuja."

"Why? So soon? He should be given a leave. He's on his honeymoon!" he teased.

Nneoma made an awkward face. She turned her head as if to see whether anybody was still around, eavesdropping on their conversation. The action made both of them laugh at the same time. She had yet to get used to the fact that she was now a married woman and no longer a girl aspiring to become a nun.

"He went to attend to an important official assignment that needed his urgent attention. Don't forget that he stayed two weeks at home. One week before the wedding and one week after the wedding."

"No, that's not enough …"

"Ehenn! Kachi … about Njideka," she interrupted him, deliberately diverting attention to a subject matter that would have been reserved for later discussion. She didn't want him to continue with the honeymoon topic. Njideka was among the cardinal subjects of her planned discussion with Onyekachi.

At the mention of Njideka, Onyekachi's countenance automatically changed. It was like opening an old wound. He became gloomy instantly.

"Nneoma," he told her in a calm voice, "I think it will do us some good if you forget everything—and I mean *everything*—about Njideka."

"Kachi, you know it is not possible. Consider all that we shared, the unequalled closeness that existed between the three of us. Consider the dreams. The dreams that were reflected in the promises you and Njideka made to each other. That is why you both must reconcile— to keep those dreams alive and bring them to reality."

"My dear, dreams are like unborn babies. Some are born hale and hearty, thereby bringing joy and celebration into the household; some are born disabled, with no enthusiasm; some are stillborn, bringing sorrow and regret; while some are cruelly aborted by their own mothers, who are supposed to sustain their lives."

"Kachi, you sound deep!"

"Yes, my dear, because you may have been underestimating this as I have not been telling you much on the current state of things between Njideka and me. This is to keep you from getting too hurt. The Njideka I loved, cherished so much, and respected so much has now turned out to be the greatest anguish of my heart. The Njideka that promised to always love me and never break my heart now tells me that those promises were childhood fantasies. The decent and disciplined Njideka, who vowed to maintain her dignity as a woman, now flirts with the so-called bigger boys on campus, who have cars and more material things to offer. She now refers to me as a 'childhood friend.' Njideka has shattered my heart. I think the best thing for me is to erase her completely from my memory."

"I'm sorry, really sorry, Kachi. But you didn't tell me all this previously."

"It's because I don't like discussing Njideka anymore, and like I said, I didn't want you to feel too hurt because of her actions. Talking about her or even remembering her is like trying to swallow the bitter pill all over again ... and again!"

"That's too bad! That explains why she's been avoiding me. She even refused after I took the time to visit her with a special invitation to be my chief bridesmaid. I didn't meet her that day, but now I know that she deliberately avoided me. It was almost at the eleventh hour, when it was so obvious that she would not come, that I got somebody to replace her."

"Yes, and that's why I want you to see Njideka as history—history that is not good to be discussed at all!"

"And, Kachi, you said that dreams are like unborn babies. I think there are still other types of such unborn babies."

"Yes, I know about that too. I think we have to add here that some are expected to be born as baby boys while they turned out eventually being born as baby girls, or vice versa. I hope I spoke your mind, Mrs. Max Nwigwe."

She made a face.

Chapter 15

"*Ejoo ... ejoo ...,*" Adekunle besought the *danfo* bus driver in his local dialect, which meant "please," rubbing his palms together. The danfo bus was a mini bus used for commercial transportation to carry passengers. It was only after he had already swerved his car partially in front of the danfo bus, risking a dent.

"*Oya wole,*" the danfo bus driver signaled as he urged him forward. Daring the consequence and to maintain his earlier position ahead of Adekunle, the danfo driver could have gone ahead to attempt hitting Adekunle's car. Danfo bus drivers often behaved that way.

Adekunle entered the lane ahead of him. It was unusual that the danfo bus driver, unlike others, was not in a hurry to pick passengers ahead of other competitors. Other danfo bus drivers never left more than ten inches of space between vehicles in front of them, moving bumper-to-bumper so as not to allow any space for another vehicle to enter the lane ahead of them. In addition, when the traffic got heavier, their driving methods became more aggressive; they didn't care if they hit or dented other vehicles, and vice versa. Their manner of driving had landed some of them in trouble, yet they couldn't care less. An official driver like Adekunle, who was trained to be a defensive driver, needed guts of iron to do what he did because it was sometimes necessary to beat traffic in Lagos. Such a method of driving, including mastering the complex road networks in Lagos, could be needed if he had to take his boss to certain official engagements on time. People could be in a traffic jam for over three hours in heavy traffic.

"*E se*," he thanked, waving to show his appreciation to the danfo driver, who may not have heard him. "*Oga*," Adekunle referred to his boss using a local dialect meaning "boss," "I'm sure we shall get there on time. A short cut I'll take will connect us to Third Mainland Bridge faster so we'll get to the mainland on time."

"Yes, Ade. You've always been precise in your calculations, and that has helped us a lot!" Onyekachi acknowledged. He trusted Adekunle to take him to the venue on time for a crucial meeting at another GBI branch. Onyekachi could not have wished for any better driver than Adekunle, who also helped him with other errands.

As Adekunle veered the car onto Third Mainland Bridge, Onyekachi's mind was reflecting on his earlier ambition of becoming a civil engineer. Though he was content with what he was, he still felt a vacuum in his heart for not accomplishing his original ambition. Perhaps the only thing that would fill that vacuum was if he had a child that would become one. At the thought of his own child, his mind went back to Njideka in a flash.

The trauma he'd suffered had since gone. It was carried away as the years rolled by. Onyekachi had learned his lesson even as a full-grown man. It was a bitter lesson that made him resolve never to surrender his heart to any woman again. The love he had for Njideka was so strong that he couldn't imagine that she would not share the rest of her life with him. Each time he thought of Njideka, he pictured a heartbreaker and a cheat. He felt badly cheated. He wondered if it was wrong to keep chaste, and looked forward to a perfect union. He could easily pass for a big fool before some people. Although he'd had little or no feelings for Njideka lately, he had not completely forgotten about her. After all, she was his first love, the only girl he had loved and trusted. He did love her not in the manner, as he had with Nneoma. He often wondered whether he would be able to love another woman the way he did Njideka. Even if he prepared his mind to love another woman, would he ever trust her? He planned to marry young, and trust was extremely important in any marriage.

From his second to his final year in the university, Onyekachi distanced himself from any serious relationships with girls. Though it was common and easy to start one on campus, he never considered it a necessity. His final year was characterized by trials. He nearly lost his life on one occasion. There was a shootout between two opposing cult groups, and a stray bullet hit a student by his side. She was later confirmed dead in a hospital. His final year project involved a lot of money, and he almost starved to save money in order to execute the project. During his final semester examination, a well-known examination cheat whom Onyekachi detested tried implicating him when he was caught in malpractice, simply because he did not want to go down alone. Had it not been for the godly supervisor and other candidates who exonerated Onyekachi, it would have been a different story. His reputation and effort would have been tarnished. The cheat was later rusticated from the university.

After National Youth Service, he was able to save some money from his allowances. Things had significantly improved with Eze, who got married when he was rounding off his final year project. He had a swell time running professional certification exams with the Institute of Chartered Accountants. He had an outstanding performance and qualified as a chartered accountant. Immediately, one of the top leading new generation banks, Galaxy Bank International (GBI), hired him. He was assistant chief accountant at the bank's headquarters in

Nigeria, on Lagos Island. He was given a chauffeur-driven official car and a special accommodation allowance, which he used to rent and furnish a flat on the island.

As Adekunle pulled the car up to the door, Onyekachi caught a glimpse of a feminine figure standing by the door to his flat. As he alighted from the car, he got a clearer view. It was unmistakably Nneoma, even though she had added considerable weight.

"Kachi, my brother! Oh, it's been ages!" Nneoma exclaimed as she ran to meet him and give him a long-lasting hug.

"God bless my soul!" Onyekachi never would have expected to see Nneoma at his residence. "Nneoma, is it you that I'm hugging? No wonder they say that it is only a dead person that never resurfaces when mentioned or remembered."

Nneoma held on to Onyekachi as she sank her head into his right shoulder. Her eyes were filled with tears. "Kachi, it's me. It's Nneoma," Nneoma replied as she released her hold and lifted her face for Onyekachi to see, as if to confirm to him that it was she.

"It's all right, my dear. Don't get too emotional," Onyekachi said. "Umm … Ade! Get my briefcase in the car. Please tell Akpan my houseboy to take her bags to the guest room."

"Yes, Oga," Adekunle replied.

The last time Onyekachi had seen Nneoma was at Eze's wedding, which she had attended with her baby girl, who was then a few months old. That was about two years back. Nneoma was then a first year student of Mass Communication in the FCT University. Max had bought her a small car, which she was using to attend lectures. Nneoma and Max were compatible and brought out the best in each other as husband and wife.

Onyekachi had greatly missed Nneoma and longed to see her. His job kept him on a tight schedule, even most weekends.

"That's Junior." Nneoma gestured to a baby sleeping in a foldable mobile baby cot by the side of the entrance door. "He's three months old. My girl has a baby brother now."

Onyekachi looked at the baby and back to Nneoma, again at the baby and back to Nneoma, as if to be sure that it was really Nneoma's baby.

"Goodness gracious! God is great! What a beautiful baby!" Onyekachi stooped and pecked the baby on the cheek. He stirred and started crying. Onyekachi picked him up, holding him the way men hold babies. "Sorry, sorry, my soldier," he cooed, and Junior fell asleep again.

When they were seated in the sitting room, not a second went by that Nneoma and Onyekachi weren't deep in conversation.

"When the lack of communication with you became unbearable for me, I asked Max to go home on my behalf during his annual leave to get your address from Mama," Nneoma said.

"Good. I misplaced the Abuja address and phone number you gave me during Eze's wedding, so I couldn't contact you either. How were you able to locate my new residence? I know that people at home only have my office address for now."

"I went to your office and came across Gloria, daughter of Mazi Njoku of Umuagu, who was around to meet her husband in the bank."

"Yeah, her husband works with us in another department. They're about the only people who have my home address, and I could call them my nearest relatives around this estate." He removed his coat and loosened his tie. "So how about Max ... and your program?"

"Max traveled to New York City for a workshop that will span two weeks. His office sent him. I'm pushing my program; this is my third year."

"Any news from home lately?"

"Yes, Kachi. Good news!"

"So share the news."

Tears started coming out from Nneoma's eyes, rolling down her cheeks, leaving two parallel lines. Onyekachi became confused and wondered what good news would make her shed tears, or were they tears of joy?

"The news is that I have a living blood brother," she revealed.

"What brother are you talking about?" he asked, still confused. When he could no longer bear the sight of the flowing tears, he moved closer and held her, trying to console her. "Why are you crying? If what you're saying is so, it actually calls for a celebration rather than weeping. Pull yourself together and tell me everything."

"The baby my mother delivered before I was born was not dead, as we thought. His name is Greg. After my mother had the baby before Greg, which died immediately after birth, she decided to go to Enugu to deliver Greg and see if it would make a difference. Her elder sister, my aunt, then lived in Enugu with her husband, who worked with the National Railway Cooperation. The midwife in Enugu was briefed accordingly of her previous experiences. The midwife, who was childless, capitalized on that and reported that baby Greg died shortly after birth too. In their grief, my mother and my aunt believed it was the usual sad story and never even bothered to see the supposedly dead baby.

"The midwife kept the baby and gave him the best any parent could give a child. Greg is now a medical doctor. She was being haunted by what she did, and she had to confess to Greg. Greg insisted that the only way he'd forgive her was for her to trace his roots. This wasn't easy because my aunt and her husband had since left Enugu, after her husband's retirement. Finally, as God would have it, she got help with records at the office of National Railway Corporation in Enugu."

"Wonders shall never end!" Onyekachi exclaimed.

"I think you should hear this too: Uncle Jonah is dead. He died two months before this discovery. He was struck by a strange disease and was in deep pain. But before he died, he made the biggest confession of all time. He admitted responsibility for most of the deaths in my family, including my father's."

"Jeee-sus!" Onyekachi screamed. "Which means that your brother survived because he thought he was dead already, and in your case, maybe he felt you were no threat to him since you are a girl?"

Tears were flowing from her eyes again, and Onyekachi stood up and produced a handkerchief from his pocket, which she used to dry them as much as she could. He sat down again and consoled her.

"I believe that wherever your father and mother are now, they are happy because Greg and you will keep their names remembered."

"Greg promised to come home. Now he's planning to move his base to Abuja to be closer to me." Nneoma said, sobbing.

The next morning was one of those rare Saturdays that Onyekachi didn't have to work. Breakfast had been served on the dining table. While he watched *Weekend Breakfast Ride* on the television set, he waited for Nneoma, who was attending to Junior in the guest room, to join him for breakfast. There was a knock on the door.

"Akpan!" Onyekachi called. "Please get the door."

Akpan moved toward the nearby window and peered.

"Oga, it's a woman," he announced to Onyekachi, the "g" in the word "oga" sounded like "k" with his accent.

"Really? Okay, let her in," Onyekachi directed. Even though he was curious and wanted to see her, he was almost certain that the stranger had the wrong address.

As she walked into the sitting room, he faced her again: the woman who, as a teenage girl, stole his heart and decorated it with love; who also broke his heart in no small measure, made him suffer much, and taught him the most bitter lessons of love. She looked as gorgeous as ever and seemed well-off, too.

"Can I sit down?" she requested, reenacting her politeness and humility, which in the past had captured his heart a great deal.

"You may sit down," he replied. After a brief pause, he asked, "Who gave you my address? Who told you that I live in Lagos?"

"It doesn't matter, does it?" she said. "It's a small world, you know?"

"To what do I owe this visit?" he asked without further delay, sounding formal.

"I've come to settle the score with you, Kachi. My life will know no peace if I don't make peace with you."

"I've forgiven you, though difficult initially, and I want to assure you that there is no war between us."

"Thank you very much, Kachi. But I also want you to realize that this is much more than just asking forgiveness. We ..."

"Skip it! Save your breath. So much water has gone under the bridge. Sorry, I have no feelings for you, and you can never be the same girl I used to know."

"Yes, Njideka," Nneoma intervened, carrying her baby as she entered the sitting room. "For crying out loud, you cannot have your cake and eat it too! You surprise me. Are there no more happening guys around? He will not need you in his life again. I don't have to be a prophetess to tell you, do I?"

Nneoma noticed that Njideka was visibly shaken. She'd never expected to meet her ... and her baby. She looked at her baby, who smiled back in return. There was a brief moment of silence, and Junior began to cry, as if he did not like the silence. Nneoma went to the guest room to fetch the baby formula. Njideka stood and turned to leave but, as if considering a second thought, turned back and drew closer to Onyekachi, who was also standing. She looked straight into his eyes.

"I know I have misbehaved grossly, which I find difficult to explain why—perhaps there'll be an explanation sometime. I am not even worthy to stand before you with any excuses whatsoever because of the betrayal and trauma I caused you over the years. But maybe it's absolutely necessary, and that I have to forgive myself too, even as I hope I will get a second chance.

"Kachi, there is something I have ... something I've fought hard to keep all these years. I have kept it even during those years of my bizarre madness, consciously or unconsciously ... or by divine arrangement. No man has ever touched it. I think I would be right to say that it belongs to only one man. I think it belongs to you. And let me be damned and never be forgiven by Heaven if I've come to deceive you."

He had not known her as somebody who used too much emphasis to prove a point. To introduce God into it meant more.

"What are you talking about, Njide?"

"You know what I'm talking about."

What Onyekachi thought was a closed chapter wasn't after all. He was beginning to learn that the world was full of still more irony. Although he found the irony difficult to understand, it was set to bring him to the realization of one of the most beautiful dreams he'd ever had: the dream to be united with Njideka forever.